LOVE IS IN THE AIR

fLiRT

Also in the Flirt series:

Lessons in Love

Never Too Late

Portrait of Us

Sunset Ranch

Puppy Love

LOVE IS IN THE AIR

A. DESTINY AND ALEX R. KAHLER

SIMON PULSE

NEW YORK   LONDON   TORONTO   SYDNEY   NEW DELHI

SIMON PULSE

An imprint of Simon & Schuster Children's Publishing Division

1230 Avenue of the Americas, New York, New York 10020

First Simon Pulse paperback edition February 2015

Text copyright © 2015 by Simon and Schuster, Inc.

Cover photograph copyright © 2015 by Westend 61/Getty Images

All rights reserved, including the right of reproduction in whole or in part in any form.

SIMON PULSE and colophon are registered trademarks of Simon & Schuster, Inc.

For information about special discounts for bulk purchases, please contact Simon & Schuster Special Sales at 1-866-506-1949 or business@simonandschuster.com.

The Simon & Schuster Speakers Bureau can bring authors to your live event. For more information or to book an event contact the Simon & Schuster Speakers Bureau at 1-866-248-3049 or visit our website at www.simonspeakers.com.

Book design by Regina Flath

The text of this book was set in Adobe Caslon Pro.

Manufactured in the United States of America

10 9 8 7 6 5 4 3 2 1

Library of Congress Cataloging-in-Publication Data

Destiny, A.

Love is in the air / by A. Destiny and Alex R. Kahler.

pages cm.—(Flirt)

Summary: When fifteen-year-old Jennifer attends circus camp to reach her dream of being a trapeze artist, she learns she is afraid of heights, but after one glimpse of Branden, the best trapeze artist at the camp, Jennifer begins falling for him, too.

[1. Camps—Fiction. 2. Circus—Fiction. 3. Love—Fiction. 4. Fear—Fiction.]

I. Kahler, A. R. II. Title.

PZ7.D475Lo 2015

[Fic]—dc23

2014030468

ISBN 978-1-4814-2376-2 (pbk)

ISBN 978-1-4814-2378-6 (eBook)

Chapter ◕ One

Ever since I was a little girl, I've dreamed of being a star on the flying trapeze. Most girls grow up wanting to be a ballerina or a princess. Most of them stop dreaming once they become a teenager. Not me. Ever since my parents took me to see my first circus show, I knew that that was the life for me. Watching the aerialist flip and twirl in midair, listening to all that applause . . . I couldn't think of anything better. Everyone in the tent was watching; everyone wanted to be them. And someday I wanted to be the one who was the source of all that admiration.

Of course, it's hard to run away and join the circus when your parents are dead set on you going to college—probably for something practical like accounting or dentistry. It also doesn't help when you live in the Middle of Nowhere, Missouri.

So the fact that I'm here, standing in front of a sign reading THE KARAMAZOV SISTERS' TRAVELING CIRCUS: FIRST ANNUAL YOUTH CAMP, is a pretty big deal. I mean, the Karamazov Sisters have been coming to town every summer for as long as I can remember. But them having a circus camp? One where I could learn flying trapeze and become a star? It almost seems too good to be true.

"You owe us for the rest of your life," my mom says. "Remember this, Jennifer, when you're picking out our nursing home."

I grin at her and Dad.

"I know," I say. Neither of them really wanted me to go to camp. I think they would rather I'd have just stayed at home and played video games with my friends like I had every other spring break. But I'm fifteen. It's time to start reaching for my dreams. And a weeklong camp doing circus is the best way to begin. I know, deep down, that this is going to be life-changing. This is the point in my story where I finally flourish. At least, that's what I've been telling myself right up to now.

Actually being here is starting to make me worry that I might have been wrong about all that.

The camp is held on the community college campus. We stand in the parking lot in front of the main office, and it's hard to believe that I've biked past here more often than I can count. The place is entirely different, and not just because there are dozens of teenagers my age walking around with their parents.

There are semitrucks parked outside the gym, and there are tents being put up. None of them are quite as big as the big top for the Karamazov show, but they're all genuine circus tents, stripes and stars and all. My heart leaps when I see the structure they're assembling a little farther off, out on the soccer field. It's not complete, but I know without a doubt what it is.

"Looks like that's where you'll be spending all your time," Dad says, noticing my gaze. He's got my suitcase balanced against his leg. I didn't pack much, since it's only for a week. And besides, gymnastics clothes—all new, all part of my early birthday present—pack up pretty easily.

I don't actually have words. I stare at the flying trapeze rig, a little starstruck, and nod.

I'm not left to stare long. A girl who looks like she's a college supermodel comes up to us. She's got long brown hair in a ponytail and impeccable makeup. Her green eyes match the T-shirt she's wearing, and her shorts barely reach her thigh. She's gorgeous. What's more, I've seen her before; she's one of the hoop aerialists for the show.

"Hi," she says, stopping in front of me. She holds out her hand with a warm smile. "I'm Leena. Are you here for the camp?"

I nod as I take her hand, unable to peel my eyes from her. Just last summer I was watching this girl perform amazing stunts on a hoop dangling a dozen feet in the air. And now she's shaking my hand! It's like meeting a celebrity, only this star's hands are covered in calluses, and there are a few bruises on her forearms and calves.

"Did you get attacked by a lion?" my dad asks. I shoot him the angriest look I can manage. I haven't even gotten to introduce myself yet.

3

The girl raises an eyebrow, then looks to her arms and laughs.

"No, though that would make for a better story. These are just part of the gig. The battle scars of being an aerialist. Turns out hanging from a metal hoop hurts." She laughs again. "I'm sorry, I shouldn't be scaring you off. Especially not before getting your name."

"Jennifer," I say. "Jennifer Hayes. And these are my parents."

Leena shakes my mom's and dad's hands, and I can tell from my mom's expression that she's not too happy about the fact that this girl is covered in bruises from being in the circus. At least she doesn't say anything; she's a little more tactful than Dad.

"Nice to meet you, Jennifer," Leena says. "Is this your first time doing circus arts?"

I nod. Even though she's at least twenty-one, there isn't any condescension in her voice. She's looking at me like even if I'm not currently her equal, I might be. Someday.

"Well, this is going to be an intense week. I hope you're ready for it. You look like you're a natural, though—nothing to worry about." She gives me a grin. "Anyway, registration's right inside the door. They'll get you sorted and into your dorm. I'll see you at the opener in an hour."

She nods to my parents and then walks off toward another group of kids milling about as aimlessly as I probably appear to be.

"She seems nice," my dad says when she's out of earshot.

"Yeah," I say. I'm still glowing. A natural? She thinks I could be a natural? "Really smooth, by the way. Thanks for trying to embarrass me."

"I wasn't," he replies. "I just wanted to make sure she hadn't been hurt, that's all. I mean, I'm entrusting you to her care. If there's anything bad going on behind the scenes . . ."

"I know, I know." I pat him on the arm. "You gotta look out for your little girl."

"You're sure you want to do this aerial thing?" Mom asks. She keeps glancing back to Leena, no doubt wondering if there are more bruises we can't see. "It looks . . . painful."

"Totally sure," I say. "Besides, she does hoop. I'm going to do flying trapeze—the only thing I have to worry about are bad calluses. Come on. Before registration closes."

I head toward the door. They stay behind, but only for a moment. Then they're following at my heels, the wheels of my suitcase rumbling on the pavement. The sky is clear, it's not crazy hot outside, and I've just met one of my new coaches—who I've been watching for years. I don't think this day could get any better if it tried.

Registration is quick and simple; not ten minutes later, my parents are hugging me outside the door to my dorm room, which is actually just one of the rooms in on-campus housing. There aren't any tears shed, not like when I went to my first and only summer camp four years ago. I mean, I'm only here a week, and my house is only a few miles away. I think I can cope. Or if I'm being really honest here, I think *they* can cope.

"Call if you need anything," Dad says.

"And make sure you text us when you know the time for your show. We wouldn't miss it for the world."

"I will," I say. I hug them both. "Love you."

Then, just like that, they're gone. Vanished down the hall. And I'm sitting in my room, staring at a suitcase of leotards and shorts and sweatpants, about to start the first day of the rest of my life. I've done it. I've basically run away and joined the circus, at least for a week. I grin. No more "Jennifer Hayes, girl no one really paid attention to." It's time for "Jennifer Hayes, high-flying circus star" to take the stage.

The door opens again a few minutes later, when I'm putting my clothes away in one of the drawers. I glance over. The first thing I notice is fire-engine red. Then I realize the shock of red is attached to the head of a girl. I blink hard. Yep, her hair is bright red, the same color as the striped red-and-black stockings sticking out of her camo skirt.

"Hi," she says the moment she's in the room. "You must be my roommate. I'm Riley."

"Jennifer," I say. "You're not from around here, are you?"

Because I'd have remembered a girl with bright-red hair and crazy clothes. This isn't a town where people try to stick out. I think they just save that for when they run off to college.

She shakes her head, making her puffy red hair fly. She's got deep-brown eyes the same color as mine, and she's roughly my same height and size. And that's in her clunky gunmetal-gray boots, too.

"Nope," she says, dropping her bags by the free bed. She's

carrying two bags, another slung over her shoulder. "I'm about an hour away. Near Jefferson City."

"Lucky," I say. "Welcome to the Middle of Nowhere. Your nightly entertainment will be an old movie theater that only plays movies already on DVD and an arcade with one working pinball machine."

She laughs and hauls a suitcase—black with pink stars—onto her bed. "Sounds like a fun place to grow up."

"It's a place to grow up," I say. "But I guess I can't complain; we got the circus after all."

"I know!" She slides the small duffel bag from her back; it's incredibly lumpy and covered in bumper stickers saying everything from DON'T TEMPT DRAGONS TO SAVE THE HUMANS! "I've been waiting all school year for this."

I've known her less than five minutes, and I can already tell she's going to be a fun roommate. When she starts pulling juggling pins and stringless tennis rackets from her bag, my thoughts are confirmed.

"Let me guess," I say. I flop down on my bed and watch her unpack her bag of tricks. "You're a juggler?"

"How could you tell?" she asks. "Was it the hair?"

"Totally. Jugglers always have weird hair."

"Goes with the territory. What about you? What's your focus?"

"Flying trapeze," I say. No hesitation.

"Really? Huh."

"What?"

"It's just that I didn't know they had a flying trapeze school here."

"They don't," I say slowly. And that's when it dawns on me: She's already a juggler. She's been doing this for years. Crap.

"Oh," she says. She stops rummaging through her bag and sits on her bed, facing me. There's barely three feet between us—I don't know how two college kids can live in here for a full year. "Have you done classes somewhere else?"

"Nope. It's just something I've always wanted to do."

She nods. "I don't mean to be rude, but you do know you have to try out for that department, right?"

"Yeah, I know," I say. "I saw it in the flyer. But, I dunno. I've always wanted to do it. It sounds stupid, but I guess I just know it's something I'll be good at." I decide not to tell her that Leena said I looked like a natural—I'm starting to think maybe the girl was just being nice.

She shrugs. "Not stupid. I felt that way about juggling and learned a basic three-ball pass in five minutes."

"I . . . honestly, I have no idea what that means."

Her grin goes wider. Her cheeks are covered in freckles; she looks like one of those girls who's used to smiling a lot.

"I'll show you," she says. She digs into her bag beside her and pulls out six multicolored juggling balls. "A three-ball pass is the basic juggling form," she says. Then she tosses three to me.

"Oh, I don't juggle," I say, though now that I think of it, I don't think I've actually ever tried before.

"Come on," she says. "You gotta try at least."

My first impulse is to say, *No, that's okay, I just want to see you try*. But that's the old Jennifer. Today, right now, I'm Jennifer reinvented, and I'm not going to turn down any opportunity. I mean, how many times in my life do I have the chance to be taught juggling by a girl with fire-engine hair? I pick up the balls from where they landed on the bed and watch her.

"Okay, it goes like this. Start with two balls in one hand, one in the other. I always start with two in the right because I'm right-handed, but everyone's different."

I follow her lead and put two in my right hand.

"Now, you're going to toss the one from your right hand into the air, trying make its apex just above eye level. Like this." She tosses the ball up in a perfect arc, its peak right below her hairline, and catches it without even moving her left hand. "You try."

I do. And much to my surprise, it's a pretty good toss. The ball lands just beside my left hand.

"Nice," she says. I smile. "Okay, now for the second toss. Don't try to catch it just yet. You want to throw the ball in your left hand when the first ball is at its peak. Once you've done that, you're going to throw the third ball when the second is at its peak. Got it?"

I nod. "I think so."

She demonstrates, tossing her balls up in a steady rhythm and letting them fall on the bed. I mimic her.

"Nice," she says again. "I think you've got the hang of it. Now we try it with the catch. Remember, you don't want to have to move your hands around too much, and you definitely don't want to throw the balls forward or back, or else you'll be running all over the place trying to catch them. Always throw the next ball when the other has reached the apex. Rinse and repeat."

She picks up the balls and tosses them in the air a few times, making clean catches and tosses—the balls are a blurred arc in front of her face. I lose track of how many times she tosses before she stops and looks at me.

"Your turn."

I try.

The first few catches are a disaster—I'm so focused on catching the ball that I forget to toss the next. When I do remember, I end up throwing it at the closed window. Thankfully, the balls are just Hacky Sacks, so the window doesn't break. I have to give Riley credit: She doesn't laugh at all. Just watches me and gives me little pointers like, "Don't move your torso so much" or "You're not trying to hit the ceiling! It's a gentle toss."

After about five minutes, she stops watching me and goes back to unpacking. I'm hooked, though, and I don't stop practicing. Not until I've managed six tosses in a row. And that takes a good ten minutes.

"Not bad," she says. She managed to unpack everything in the time it took me to get the pass down. "You're definitely starting to get it." She glances at her watch. "Just in time, too. I think we've got the intro meeting in a few minutes. Do you have any idea where the gym is?"

I nod. "Yeah, I've been there a few times. My mom used to be a secretary here, and we went to a few games."

"Funny. I wouldn't peg you for a basketball sort of girl."

"I'm not. Band nerd all way. But I'll never say no to free popcorn and an excuse to watch a bunch of college boys running around."

Her smile is huge.

"We're going to be good friends, Jennifer," she says. She hops off the bed and takes my elbow with hers, prom style.

"Definitely."

Chapter ✿ Two

The gym is nothing at all like I remember from the games. The bleachers have all been folded back against the wall, making the space seem twice as big as it usually is. But that's not what makes the room look so strange. Half the room is covered in blue tumbling mats, the other half lined with unicycles and large metal hoops bigger than I am tall. I'm assuming the people in green T-shirts with KARAMAZOV CIRCUS emblazoned on the back are the coaches; they're the ones setting everything up, and a few are even practicing as the rest of the campers filter in and huddle by the entrance. Coaches run up and down the length of the tumbling mats, doing flips and cartwheels and other tricks I don't have names for. One coach is on one of the big hoops—he spins around on it like a coin tossed on the ground, dancing about like it's the easiest thing in the world.

In that moment, I'm incredibly grateful for Riley's presence. The kids around me are all strangers. The coaches are all older and more impressive than should be humanly possible. And I suddenly have the terrible feeling that everyone in this room has been doing this for a lot longer than I have, not that that would take much. I'm probably the only one without an ounce of experience. I'm an imposter. And if not for Riley's comforting arm in mine—and her previous encouraging compliments still ringing in my ear—I'd have turned around and called home.

I look over to the girls clustered a few feet to my left. The three of them are wearing matching blue hoodies and shorts, their blond hair pulled back in ponytails. They're ridiculously skinny and have that sort of stature that says they practice ballet—chin up, shoulders back, feet turned out. Definitely sisters. Or if they're not, they're some sort of *Twilight Zone* anomaly.

"I don't think they're human," comes a voice behind me. Riley and I turn around.

The boy standing there is a little taller than me, and he's gorgeous. He's wearing a loose lavender T-shirt and a beanie cap over his curly black hair. He's tan and clearly goes to the gym. Often. But he's not bulky like the wrestlers or football jocks at my school—he looks like a swimmer.

"Tyler," he says, holding out his hand. I shake it. I can't stop the blush rising in my cheeks. His smile is infectious, and he doesn't take his brown eyes off me while we shake.

"I'm Jennifer," I squeak.

"A pleasure," he responds.

When Riley takes his hand and introduces herself, though, his attention shifts smoothly to her. Maybe that's just how he looks at people—with his full attention, none of that eye sliding most people do. I can't help but think that this somehow makes him infinitely more attractive.

"What do you think?" he asks, his voice dropped to a whisper. He nods to the blond girls. "Genetic experiments gone wrong or cyborgs?"

I snort and try to cover it with a normal laugh. It fails, obviously, but it just makes him smile. So much for being smooth around the cute new guy.

"Cyborgs," I whisper. "Definitely."

Riley eyes the girls warily. "I've heard of them. They call themselves the Twisted Triplets. They're contortionists. They went to nationals for gymnastics last year."

"If they're that good, what are they doing here?" I ask.

"Heck if I know," she replies. "They should be, like, training for the Olympics or something."

We don't have time to ask any more questions, because at that moment the coach from earlier, Leena, steps up to the crowd.

"Hey, everyone!" she calls out. The campers quiet down immediately. Riley takes my arm again and Tyler sidles up to my left, blocking the Twisted Triplets from view. "I'm Leena," she continues, "and I'm the lead aerial coach for this session. All of us coaches are really excited for this week—we can't wait to meet and train each and every one of you. But since there are a lot of you and a lot of us, we thought the best way to do introductions was to put together a little show. So, first we're going to show you what we do, and then you can show us what you do. If you want to, of course." She grins. "There's no pressure, and you'll all get your chance to shine during the show at the end of the session. So, if you all want to have a seat over there, we'll get started!"

She guides us over to a spot along the rolled-in bleachers and we sit down in rows. Tyler's arm is brushing mine, and Riley's knee is against my leg. Save for the butterflies fluttering around at Tyler's touch, it feels like we're all old friends—the closeness seems pretty natural.

Once we're all seated, Leena jogs over to join the coaches lined up along the opposite wall. Then she claps her hands three times in a steady beat, and the show begins with a fanfare.

Music blares through the loudspeakers as the coaches jog toward us, some of them flipping and cartwheeling as they go. I start clapping immediately along to the music, and I'm not the only one. Tyler and Riley are clapping along too, and soon all the campers are joining the beat.

Long strips of fabric unroll from the ceiling, and a few girls and guys start climbing. Below them, five coaches are doing some crazy sort of acrobatics; they run toward and up one another, flipping and tossing themselves and their partners up and around in dizzying flips and crazy handstands. The people on the aerial fabric pose in backbends and drop into death-defying rolls as two guys pull out the large metal hoops along the wall and begin rolling around each other like coins in a dance that makes me wonder if they'll crash. It's chaos in its coolest form. People are juggling and flipping and doing handstands and dropping from the ceiling and then, after only a few minutes, they all do one final trick and line up, facing us. They give a bow and call out their names: "I'm Brad and I teach Cyr wheel!" "I'm Tori and I teach acrobatics!"

They all sound a little winded, but not nearly as bad as I would have been.

I'm only a little disappointed that there wasn't any flying trapeze, but I guess I can't expect them to set that up in the gym. A few of the coaches call out that they teach flying trap, but I think I saw them doing acrobatics on the ground. Clearly, they expect everyone to do a little bit of everything. I'm just hoping I can do even *one* thing that impressive.

One of the coaches steps forward. She looks a little older than the others, but she's still built like a super gymnast and could probably outrun anyone in my school. Her hair is pulled back in a bun, and if I remember right, she was one of the aerialists. I don't recognize her until she speaks—Olga Karamazov looks a lot different without all the stage makeup. I actually think she looks better without it.

"Greetings, campers!" she says. Her voice is laced with a thick Russian accent, but years under the American big top have washed some of it away. "And welcome to the first annual Karamazov Circus Camp. I know you're all as excited as we are for this week;

the days will be long and the work will be hard, but together we will create an amazing show and even more amazing memories. My name is Olga Karamazov, and my sister and I created this company ten years ago. Sadly, she is down in Florida training, but I am delighted to be working with such a fantastic group of coaches to teach you all. I can assure you that each member has been handpicked not only for their skills, but for their character. Although proper technique and safe training are our top priorities, we want to ensure that you have fun while performing! After this afternoon's presentation, we will do a small series of team-building exercises so you can learn even more about one another. Then, tomorrow, you'll have your auditions. I'm sure all of you have ideas of what you'd like to train in, and I want to let you know that we will do our best to give you your first choice. Coaches aren't just looking for skill and aptitude, they're looking for a willingness to learn. So if you're new to this, don't worry. Remember, fun is the name of the game—this is a circus, after all!"

She flashes a big smile. It's hard to calm the nerves doing backflips in my stomach, though. I've been daydreaming about trying out on the flying trapeze for months—heck, for years—but now that it's here, I'm kind of terrified. Suddenly the idea of being that high up makes my head reel with vertigo.

"Speaking of fun, I think it's time for you to take the stage! You're welcome to come up and show off a few tricks or a routine if you have one. Our coaches will be watching and spotting from the sidelines, but please—no tricks you aren't entirely comfortable with. We don't want any injuries before the training even begins!"

At that, all the coaches save for Leena walk to the sides of the auditorium. Olga asks us to come up one by one—"But again, only if you want!"—and tell our name and a bit about ourselves, including what we're planning on auditioning for and how long we've been doing circus arts.

In that moment, I promise myself that I will not, under any circumstances, go up there. I mean, what would I do? Try to juggle? Do a cartwheel?

I'm not at all surprised that the Twisted Triplets are the first to stand. They stride to the center of the auditorium and position themselves on the panel mat. When they face us, they're so poised, I feel like I'm watching a professional show—even if they are just wearing hoodies and shorts. One of them sets an MP3 player and speakers down. Of course they have a routine prepared. And of course they always carry the equipment to show it off.

Even though I haven't even spoken to them yet, I don't like these girls. And I'm about 80 percent certain it's not out of jealousy, either.

"We're the Twisted Triplets," the shortest blond-haired girl says. Oddly enough, she has a really thick Southern accent. Something about her appearance made me think she'd be Ukrainian or something exotic like that. She could be my neighbor, for all I know. "We've each been trained in contortion and rhythmic gymnastics since we were three. We're hoping your coaches will be able to teach us something new, 'cause we're getting bored of our old routine. Which is what we're going to show y'all now."

She nods to her other sisters, and the tallest one, who looks older, hits play on the MP3 player, then runs to line up with the rest—they are definitely not triplets, by the way. Seconds later the gym is flooded with bass and synths as some strange mashup of techno and pop music bursts through the room. But the music is nothing compared to what starts happening onstage.

"Are they . . . stripping?" Tyler whispers incredulously in my ear.

"I think so," I say. Because as one, the girls start sashaying around and undoing the zippers of their hoodies. I almost close my eyes out of embarrassment for them, but then I catch the sparkle of unitards underneath. In one quick swish, they peel out of their hoodies to reveal spangled pink spandex. From the corner of my eye I can see Leena, who's watching the girls like she might stop them at any moment. Like the rest of us, I don't think she quite believes what she's seeing.

Thankfully, after the introduction, the awkwardness shifts into something that looks a little more like an award-winning gymnastics routine. Two of the sisters do back walkovers and pause in handstands, flattening their backs until they were parallel to the ground. The shortest then steps on the backs of her sisters, reaches down, and does a handstand on their necks, balancing between them like the Eiffel Tower. No one applauds. Not because it isn't good, but because it's just so . . . unexpected.

I don't have any idea how long their routine is, but after a few minutes they do some complicated backbend-headstand thing. They pose and the music stops. A beat of silence follows their dismount and bow. Then the coaches start to clap, and the rest of us join in with only a slight hesitation. The sisters have fixed, plastic grins on their faces, and their chests heave a bit with exertion.

Leena steps forward, still clapping, though she's having a hard time keeping that confused/concerned look off her face.

"That was . . . very entertaining," she says. It sounds like a question. "It's clear you've practiced that one quite a bit; I'm sure our coaches are going to have a great time working with you." I don't miss the glance she casts back to two of the coaches in the corner—one a burly man and one a short old woman—and their shared expression of disbelief.

The triplets leave the stage, grabbing their speakers as they go, and Leena calls for the next performer.

A few different campers go up. One girl does stunt-bike-style tricks on a unicycle. A boy juggles a half-dozen bowler hats. Then Tyler stands up and grabs a wooden chair from along the wall, dragging it toward the center of the room.

"I think he likes you," Riley whispers when Tyler's out of earshot.

"I think you're crazy," I reply. Because I saw how he was watching the boy doing flips and break-dance moves: the exact same way that I was. I'm pretty certain Tyler plays for the other team.

Tyler sets the chair down and stands on top of it, right before grasping the edge of the chair. Seconds later, he folds up into a perfect handstand. He twists and turns and poses, even doing some tricks on one hand. When he finally stands upright, the room explodes into applause. A lot of people release breath they didn't realize they were holding. I'm definitely one of them.

"That was amazing," I tell him when he sits back down. There's a light sheen of sweat on his face, but he's beaming in spite of—or because of—the exertion.

"Thanks," he says. "I've been training for a long time. Normally I do them on special chairs stacked on top of each other. My current limit is eight high, but I'm shooting for ten by the end of camp."

I can only stare at him. The idea of doing handstands on the back of eight chairs makes my heart hammer with fear. Crap. If the idea of a few stacked chairs makes me cringe, how the heck am I going to be able to climb the trapeze ladder? I force myself to take deep, calming breaths. I tell myself it will all be okay—I'm going to be a trapeze star. I know it. Otherwise, why am I here in the first place?

"Wow," Riley whispers. I glance over, thinking maybe she's talking about what Tyler just said about the chairs. But no, she's staring at the boy who's walking to the center of the mat.

"I'm Branden," he tells the group. "I've been training in flying trapeze for about three years, but I also do some ground work. So I figured I'd show what I've been working on, if I can borrow a Cyr wheel?"

I melt the moment I look at him. He's got short brown hair

spiked up at the front and is wearing plaid shorts and a tank top. His biceps are probably the size of my neck. Like Tyler, though, he looks built for a purpose, rather than just muscular to show off.

And he does flying trapeze, which means we'll be working together.

"I think I'm in love," I whisper, not really meaning to say it aloud. Tyler snorts with barely contained laughter.

One of the burly coaches I saw spinning around in the large steel hoops steps forward, rolling a hoop—I'm guessing that's a Cyr wheel—beside him. Branden thanks him and takes the wheel in his hands, rolls it back and forth a few times like he's testing its weight or diameter or something. Then, without even pausing to collect himself, he spins on his heel and brings the hoop with him, hopping onto the bottom rung and twisting like a penny.

Branden rotates fast and slow, alternating between the two with a dancer's grace. At one point, he lifts both legs up in the air and spins like Superman from the top of the hoop, the entire thing flashing silver under the lights of the gym. That's the only big trick—a few spins later, he stops with a slight stumble and grins. The camp applauds with the same enthusiasm as they did for Tyler's routine.

"Thanks," he says and walks the wheel over to the wall.

"Someone's crushing," Riley says.

I nudge her in the ribs; Branden's walking back over, and the last thing I need is for him to overhear something like that. I'm already bad at being smooth around guys: I don't need Riley or

Tyler making it worse. When I cast a quick glance at him, my heart leaps to see that he's looking at me, too. He catches my eye, and maybe it's my imagination, but it looks like he blushes as he grins and sits down. I quickly look away.

"And it looks like you're not the only one," Tyler taunts. I glare at him.

I don't know how I've only known these two for barely an afternoon, but they're already settling into the familiar friend routine. I grin in spite of myself; I kind of expected I'd be the outcast here. The fact that I've already found these two makes me think it's going to be an even better camp than I expected.

I can barely pay attention to the rest of the kids who go on to perform. There are jugglers and acrobats, a girl who hulas twelve hoops, and even a couple of guys doing a clown act. I try to watch them. Really. But I keep glancing over at the back of Branden's head and feeling the butterflies swarm.

Yes. This camp is going to be much better than expected. But first, I need to survive tomorrow's auditions.

Chapter ● Three

After the showcase, we're given a little more time to unpack our stuff and settle in. Riley and I stick together the entire time—back in the room, she shows me all her juggling equipment, including the purple clubs and poi (these balls-on-strings things that are swung around in intricate patterns) she said she had to special order from New England. Her bed is completely covered with clubs and scarves and balls and rings, a rainbow of different juggling equipment, and she has me try all of them out in turn. I'm still only able to do the three-ball pass she taught me earlier, but she assures me that it's really good for my first time.

"Keep this up," she says, "and you'll be better than me soon." She grins. "But then I'd have to kill you, so maybe pretend to be stupid at auditions tomorrow."

Auditions. The word sends a small jolt through me again, and I fumble the pass I was just attempting. According to the sheet that had been taped to our door, we'll be trying out for ground skills and aerial skills at different times. I first figured I'd skip trying out for a ground skill, but now that I'm seriously thinking about this flying trapeze thing, I'm wondering if it might be best to have a backup.

"You'll be okay," Riley says, catching my mood. "You're totally a natural. If you have half the skill you're showing at juggling, you'll be a master of the flying trap in no time."

Her smile is so confident, so assuring, that I don't have the heart to tell her that they're completely different skill sets, that I can't do a pull-up in gym and definitely don't do gymnastics or any number of things all the other campers seem to have in their back pockets. I keep my mouth shut, and she goes back to folding her myriad of skirts. I force myself back to juggling.

When there's a knock at the door a few minutes later, I nearly jump. But it's just Leena.

She smiles approvingly at all the juggling equipment splayed on the bed when she steps in.

"Looks like you both are settling in quite nicely," she says. Her smile is so perfect, so practiced, it's kind of hard to tell if she means it. But she honestly does look pleased by the fact that we're both practicing so early on in the game. "I didn't know you juggled as well, Jennifer."

I shrug and set the balls down. I'm surprised she actually remembered my name; there have to be at least thirty other kids here, and I know I sure wouldn't have remembered them all. "Riley just taught me," I say. "She's a really good teacher."

"I'm impressed. See? You really are a natural." Another grin, this one I'm pretty certain is real. "Anyway, I just wanted to drop in and see if you ladies needed anything. Tanya and I will be your hall counselors. Our room's at the end of the hall."

"We're okay," I say. "I don't think I've met Tanya, though."

"Oh, she's fantastic," Leena says. "She's actually one of the flying trapeze coaches, so you'll get along just fine. I'm sure you'll see her during the games tonight." The schedule had said something about team-building games, but it wasn't any more specific than that. I'm not about to ask, either. "Anyway, I'm gonna keep making introductions. I'll see you at dinner!"

"She seems nice," Riley says when the door shuts behind Leena.

"Yeah," I say. "I hope they're all like that."

Riley laughs. "Probably not—I hear the contortion coaches are really tough. But hey, we're only here a few days." There's a pause. "Speaking of, you're going to have to act fast if you want to grab that Branden kid."

Just like when I think about the flying trap, my heart skips a beat. Probably for very different reasons, though.

"I don't know what you're talking about," I lie.

"Right," she says with a laugh. "You were just drooling because you were thinking of dinner." She flops down on the bed beside me. "C'mon, he's really cute and really talented. I bet he's a really good kisser, too. You'd be stupid not to fall for him."

I blush.

"Unless you have a boyfriend already?" she asks.

I shake my head. Stupidly, I'm finding I can't actually speak. I'm still stuck on the idea of kissing Branden. More somersaults in my chest. My face flushes even hotter.

"Uh-oh," she says, rolling onto her side to stare at me. I'm pretty certain my cheeks are the same color as her hair. "I know that look."

"What look?" I ask.

"That look," she says. "You *have* had a boyfriend before, haven't you?"

"Not . . . not really." Unless you count Tony in fifth grade, who got me a stuffed bear on Valentine's Day and became so embarrassed he never talked to me again. And I definitely don't count that.

"So you've never kissed a boy either?"

I shake my head. Definitely no way I'll get my words to work for that response.

She sighs very dramatically. "It's worse than I thought," she bemoans.

"Oh, come on," I say, rediscovering my voice and giving her a little shove. "It's not that bad. Is it?" The last bit comes out as a squeak.

"No. No, definitely not. It's totally normal." Like Leena's smile, I don't believe she's being entirely honest. "But it does mean we're going to have to act fast. Branden's kind of perfect, and you're going to have to nab him before someone else does."

I bite my lip. Be more interesting than a circus girl? Like that will be an easy task.

"What about you?" I ask, trying to turn the tables. "Why don't you want to date him?"

"I'm taken," she says. She holds out her right hand—there's a tiny silver ring with a ruby on her pinkie finger. "Sandy and I have been together for almost a year now."

"Sandy?"

She hops off the bed and pulls her phone from a pocket in her duffel bag, then thumbs through the gallery until she holds it out to me. Onscreen is a gangly, mousy-haired boy with more freckles than Riley and a doofy grin on his face.

"Isn't he dreamy?" she asks.

I smile. "Totally."

"He's a stilt walker. And he juggles. We even have a partner routine together." She grins at the photo, then me, and slides the phone back in her bag. "I tell you, circus boys are the best. If you can get them to stop practicing, that is."

She looks back to me.

"This is going to be great. We're totally going to get you a boyfriend!"

I shake my head. "Good luck," I say.

"I don't need luck, I have skill. And a few tricks up my sleeve."

"What are you talking about?" I ask.

She doesn't answer, just takes my hand, pulling me off the bed.

"Time for dinner!" she says with a wink.

I interrogate her the entire way to the cafeteria, but she doesn't divulge her secret agenda. Not one bit.

Tyler meets us in the hall as we head to dinner. He hugs both of us the moment he sees us. Again, we've only known each other for an hour or so, but there's a camaraderie that feels like it's years in the making.

"How's the room?" he asks as he follows us into the cafeteria. Only half the space is in use, since there are so few of us. The other part is just storage from the rest of the year.

"Tiny," Riley says. She grins at me. "Good thing Jennifer doesn't smell bad. Otherwise it would be nasty."

"Lucky you," he replies. "I don't think my roommate knows what a shower is."

"Ew," I respond.

"You have no idea. And hopefully you never will."

Dinner that night is pretty good: roast veggies and chicken, a big pasta bake, lots of fresh bread and salads and sides, and even a huge sheet cake with the words WELCOME TO THE CIRCUS written in purple frosting. I help myself to a little bit of everything; I don't think I've had so many options in my life.

I'm so engrossed in talking to Tyler as we leave the line that I don't even realize where Riley has guided us until it's too late: right next to Branden. He's sitting at a table with a few other guys, all of them talking about some show they've just seen and the cool tricks they want to learn. I nearly drop my tray when I see him. I glare at Riley instead.

"Hey, guys," she says brightly, ignoring my furious stare. "Mind if we sit here?"

And even though I'm purposely avoiding his eyes, I can feel Branden watching me. "Sure," he says, and I'm trapped.

We sit down, and the guys all introduce themselves. I'm too busy trying not to shake or drop my tray to catch any of their names, and I'm so absorbed in the task that I don't even realize when the introductions roll around to me.

"And this is Jennifer," Riley says, coming to my rescue before I can blab out an apology. "She's actually a local, and what she lacks in eloquence she makes up for in raw talent."

I try to grin.

"What she said," I say.

It's impossible to actually pay attention to the conversation. My hands won't stop shaking as I try to eat my chicken, and taking a drink of water is embarrassing at best. Riley notices, I know— her nudge under the table is sign enough. But everyone else is either oblivious or too polite to say anything.

Until Branden stops taking part in the group's talk of who makes the best shoes for floor work and leans across the table toward me.

"So, what are you auditioning for?"

I nearly choke on my food.

"Flying trapeze," I say, and I pray it doesn't sound like the question I feel it is.

"That's awesome," he replies. "I live, like, half an hour away. Maybe we could start doing lessons together."

I glance up at him then, and his brown eyes are so intent on me I could melt under them. But maybe he's just like Tyler was when I first met him—quick to warm up, easy to show interest. There's no way this guy is interested in me. I'm definitely not impressive enough for someone like him.

"That would be cool," I say after too long a pause. I managed to forget that he was probably expecting an answer. In spite of my awkwardness, he smiles.

"How long have you been flying?" he asks.

"I haven't," I respond, and I feel my stomach sink into the floor below. "This will be my first time."

"Exciting," he says. "Everyone has a first time. And you'll remember it for as long as you live."

"What was your first time like?" I ask.

"Magical," he says. Then he laughs to himself. "And terrifying. I think I nearly passed out."

I let myself grin, but the knots in my gut just won't relax. If *he* was scared of his first leap, how in the world will I be able to manage?

"Well then, I guess you'll be in for a show tomorrow morning."

And he smiles, so maybe I'm not as hopeless as I fear I am.

"Oh, don't worry," Riley says to my left. "We'll all be there cheering you on."

I don't know if that makes me feel better or worse.

Chapter ● Four

Olga makes an announcement halfway through dinner, saying that we'll have half an hour after dinner to relax, and then it's off to team-building games. She speaks a lot about the importance of building a community in a show this size, how everyone has to be able to depend on everyone else. So she asks us to wear our name tags to the games and introduce ourselves to at least ten different people before sign-in. Then she leaves us to our dessert and goes off to drink coffee with the rest of the coaches.

"Any idea what the games are?" Branden asks us. The other guys have gone from the table, leaving just him and Tyler and Riley and me.

"No clue," Riley says, "but if it involves teams, I pick you guys."

"Deal," Branden says, and Tyler nods in agreement.

Riley opens her mouth to say something, then closes it when our table is breached by the Triplets.

The three blond girls sit down on the side with Branden, making themselves at home. None of them are carrying trays—maybe they ate already—but they each have a mug that I first think is tea, then realize is just hot water and lemon.

"Hi, there," the oldest girl says, looking straight at Branden when she says it. "I'm Megan." She holds out her hand. "It's a pleasure to make your acquaintance."

He raises an eyebrow but shakes her hand. "Branden," he replies.

"I know," she says. Then she winks at him.

Her sisters introduce themselves as Sara and Olivia, but none of them look at us when they speak. All eyes are on Branden. In fact, they don't seem to know we exist until Tyler clears his throat and introduces himself.

They practically sneer at him, but he doesn't back down, and he doesn't pull back his hand until they shake it. Then he introduces Riley and me.

"Where are you from?" Tyler asks, and I have to commend him for being civil. I kind of want to slap all of them for being so rude.

"Little Rock," Megan says.

"That's a really long way to come for just a week," I say.

Megan looks at me like I'm an idiot, and the urge to slap her comes back with a vengeance.

"No distance is too great to achieve perfection," she sneers.

Riley coughs, but I know it's to hide a laugh. It sounds like

Megan's quoting something from an inspirational poster.

Megan turns her glare to Riley, but she gets the hint. She pushes herself from the table and nods to her sisters.

"We'll see you at the games," Megan says to Branden, her sweet little smile returning in an instant. Then one more glare at us, and the Triplets leave.

"Wow," Tyler says when they're out of earshot. "They really are cyborgs."

I can't help it—I snort with laughter. Those three had me so stressed, so insecure with their good looks and confidence, that his joke is like a puncture to a balloon.

Branden chuckles as well, and soon all of us are doubled over with laughter.

When it's time to leave the cafeteria and head toward the gym for the games, Branden stays by our side. Well, by my side. I can't help but continually glance over at him while we walk. And I can't help but notice that he's doing the same.

Everyone's assembled in the gym by the time we get there. The mats have all been pushed to the sides, and the aerial equipment is pulled up into the rafters. The local radio station is playing on the sound system—one of the few stations that isn't country, thankfully—but it's hard to hear it over the sound of everyone talking. I don't know if it's intentional or not, but I find myself standing a little closer to Branden. It's like there's a static between us, a pulse pulling me closer into his orbit. We huddle in beside some of the guys from dinner—I'm pretty certain they're the acrobats, judging from how they were doing flips off one another when we walked in. I don't miss the way Tyler smiles at one of them, a short, muscular guy with red hair who introduced himself as Kevin earlier on.

"What do you think they're going to do to us?" Branden asks me through a grin.

"No clue," I respond, and Olga Karamazov steps forward before I can finish the train of thought.

"Welcome, troupers," she calls out. Her voice carries to every corner of the room, confident and strong, and the camp quiets down immediately.

"Tonight we're doing a costume challenge. To begin, we're going to break you up into teams based on your halls. If you could please find your hall counselors, we will then tell you what to do next."

"Aww," Riley says, looking to Tyler and Branden. "And here I was hoping we'd all be one happy family."

"Me too," Tyler says. "Now I'm gonna be stuck with my smelly roommate."

Riley hugs him. When she steps back, she has a wicked grin on her face. "Don't think I'll take it easy on you, girls," she says. "This is war."

Then she steps beside me and takes me by the arm, dragging me away from Branden before I can even say good-bye.

"What was that for?" I whisper to her when we're out of earshot.

"The grand exit?" she asks. "Please. You were looking at him like you were ready to propose. You need to play hard to get. Otherwise he's going to think you don't like him."

"That makes no sense," I say, sidling up to the rest of the girls in my hall.

"Boys never do," she responds. It's the most solemn thing I've heard her say all day.

We line up and my stomach does an angry little flip when I notice that Megan and the rest of the Twisted Triplets are with us. How did I miss that they were in our hall? This better not mean I have to pretend to be their friend. Megan catches my eye and gives me a wink, which she somehow manages to make full of malice. Oh yeah, we're definitely not going to be good friends. Like Riley said, this is war. I glance to Branden across the gym. If the war's over him, I better win. Though against these girls . . . I don't know if I have much of a chance.

"All right, everyone," Olga calls out. "Each hall must work as a team if you hope to win, and the winners will get a special treat before sign-in tonight.

"The way it works is simple: Each of you must dress up one of your team members according to the prompt. The other coaches will be the judge of who accomplished the task best; there *is* a time limit, and the first team to complete the task will get an extra point.

"The first look is . . . steampunk court jester. Go!"

It's an explosion of motion. Our group runs together, and in seconds we've nominated Riley to be the one who gets dressed up. Then it's off to our hall.

The hall is filled with the sounds of banging doors and slamming dressers as the rest of the girls search through their wardrobes for something that can work. I don't really have anything that fits the description, but I do have a pair of argyle leggings I just bought. Riley's grinning like the Cheshire Cat as she searches through her clothes, pulling out tutus and top hats and stage makeup. Then there's a knock on our door, and it's some girl from the hall who tells us we need to meet back at the gym. Riley and I bolt.

Everyone's laughing as Riley stands by our hall counselors and gets dressed by the rest of the hall. Megan is slapping white face paint on her while other girls button up a ringmaster coat and help her into the leggings I procured. It's impossible to keep track of time. What seems like only seconds later, Riley's running to the center of the gym. She skids to a stop before Olga, her mismatched striped socks sliding on the smooth basketball court. She's panting, but she's the first one there. Minutes later the other three halls send forth their models.

Olga blows her whistle and the gym goes quiet. Then a few of the coaches come up and start the judging.

Riley's in a red ringmaster coat with the leggings and striped socks and a skewed top hat. Someone had a necklace made of gears, so she's wearing that, and Megan managed to expertly paint a cog over Riley's left eye. Oddly enough, it looks like something Riley would wear on a normal day. Though maybe minus the face paint.

The other girl's outfit looks much more haphazard—she has starry socks on her hands, a tiger-striped leotard, a feather boa, and five watches on her arm.

Both boys did a little better than the female competition: Each is wearing a vest and a top hat, though one managed to find a pocket watch. They also both have great face paint: white with clown noses or diamonds. I'm a little disappointed to see that neither of them is Branden.

The judges take a few minutes to discuss among themselves. Then one of them whispers in Olga's ear, and she announces the winner.

"This round goes to Leena's hall, with their ringmaster court jester. Congratulations, girls. Speed and accuracy, very impressive."

Riley walks back to us with a huge grin, which looks really creepy with the face paint. Everyone slaps her on the back and hugs her, but there's not much time to celebrate; before we can figure out who the next model's going to be, Olga's calling out the next challenge.

"Summery woods fairy!"

And again, we're off. But this time it's me who's chosen to model. I have Riley to thank (or blame) for that.

The next few minutes are a blur. Riley grabs my arm and we run back to my room, trying to find anything brown or green or leafy. She throws me one of her camo skirts and a pair of brown boots, and then we're running back to the gym to see what the rest of the hall has assembled.

Megan must have appointed herself lead makeup artist, because the moment I'm standing still she rushes over and starts dusting my face with green glitter and painting swirling lines around my eyes. It's hard to even pay attention to that, because girls are wrapping me in shawls and beads and tousling my hair and then, after a whirl-wind few minutes, it's over. They push me toward Olga, and I run as fast as I can. Not fast enough, though.

I nearly stumble over my own shoelaces when I realize who beat me.

Branden is standing beside Olga. He's wearing brown pants and a brown vest, but that's not what's making it difficult to look away. He's not wearing a shirt underneath, and the rest of his team painted glittery leaves all over him. Somehow, they even got his hair green, though how they managed all that in five minutes is beyond me. He smiles when he sees me. My cheeks go hot, and I'm sud-denly very grateful for all the makeup Megan put on me.

The other two teams come up seconds later. The girl has fairy wings—who actually brought fairy wings to circus camp?—and a flowery dress and lots of glitter. The other boys' team clearly struggled: Their model is in shorts and flip-flops and a shirt with a tree on it. He smiles sheepishly when the judges come over to start the examination.

"You look good," whispers Branden. I jump when he talks. He's actually talking to *me*.

"Thanks," I manage. "You do too."

He just snickers. "Welcome to circus camp."

Moments later the judges confer with Olga. Despite this just being a silly game, my heart hammers in my chest. I suddenly really want to win this, even though I didn't have anything to do with the costume and don't even know what I look like. It's ridiculous, but I hope winning will impress Branden.

"We have a winner!" Olga announces. "Michael's team, with their glittery rendition of Puck. Well done!"

My stomach drops when it's not Leena's name. Then I realize she's talking about Branden.

"Good job!" I manage to tell him, right before we're ushered back to our groups. I watch him fist-bump his comrades when he reaches his team. A few girls clap me on the back, but it's not as warm a welcome. Especially from Megan.

"Don't even try it. I see the way you look at him," she hisses in my ear. "You don't stand a chance."

I glance at her, but she's already refocused on Olga.

"Mermaid!" Olga yells.

As Riley drags me back to our room to find something for the next look, I can't get those words out of my head. Because I know she's right. In spite of that brief bout of excitement, I don't really fit in here. I'm way too normal, too dull. And surrounded by all these glittery, amazing circus girls, I know there's no way Branden would ever pick me.

Chapter ✹ Five

You're being ridiculous," Riley says.

It's a few minutes after sign-in, and she and I are back in our dorm room. We didn't win the game—that honor went to Branden's hall and their hilarious rendition of a merman, complete with painted-on shell bra—but we did spend the last half hour chatting as a hall. Megan was giving me the evil eye the entire time. I'm surprised I didn't melt right then and there.

"I'm not," I say. I'm lying on the bed in my pj's, staring at the ceiling. One of the college kids had put up star stickers, and the RAs must have missed a few when cleaning the room; the stars glow faintly in the darkness. "I should just give up now. Megan's right—Branden would never go for me."

"So why is he being all flirty with you, huh?" she asks. She rolls on her side to look at me—even in the near dark, her fiery hair seems to glow from the corner of my eye.

I take a deep breath.

"Because it's funny."

She doesn't answer for a moment.

"What do you mean, 'it's funny'?"

"It wouldn't be the first time," I admit. I squeeze my eyes shut, like maybe it will hide me from what I'm admitting.

"What happened?" she asks. I hear her shuffle from her bed, and then she's sitting next to me, a hand on my shoulder.

"It's nothing."

"Clearly it's something."

I don't want to think about this, and I don't know why I even mentioned it. I barely know her—I don't even talk about this with the friends I've had since elementary.

"It's embarrassing," I finally admit. "But last year there was this guy. Josh. He played basketball and sat next to me in computer class. Anyway, one day he asked me out. And I said yes."

"And?"

"What do you think? He told me to meet him at this restaurant, and then he didn't show. Never gave me his number, so I just sat there, waiting, for like half an hour before I left and walked home."

"Maybe he forgot?" Riley suggests, but her voice says she already knows that's not the case.

"Nope." I try to make my own words strong, nonchalant—I've

spent the last few months convincing myself this guy didn't get to me, and it's still a struggle. "The next day he came into class, and the moment he saw me he burst out laughing. Got high fives from his friends and everything. It was . . . bad. I almost ran out of class right then. I never asked why he didn't show—must have been some sort of sick joke. You know, get the nerd girl's hopes up."

Riley doesn't answer for a while, but she also doesn't move her hand from my shoulder.

"I had something similar happen once," she finally says. "Though not with a date. Some jerk wrote me fake love notes for a week, left them in my locker. Good ones too—quoting Shakespeare and all that, so I thought they were genuine. Then the last one just said, 'JK, I would never date a girl as ugly as you.'"

I open my eyes and look at her. There's no sadness when she talks about it.

"I'm sorry," I say.

"I'm not," she responds. "It taught me that some guys are real jerks. And somehow, I dunno, after that point I just stopped caring what people thought of me." She shrugs her shoulders. "That was before I started dressing crazy—I'd spent so much time trying to fit in and look gorgeous like everyone else. I let everything go after that. And then, a few weeks later, I met Sandy at a juggling class. He liked me, fuchsia hair and all, and that's when I learned there were still gentlemen in the world, and that the important ones will like you for all your crazy." She squeezes my shoulder. "What I'm trying to say is, you can't let that one bad experience get you down. I don't think Branden's that type of guy. And if he is, screw it. There's someone out there for you. And when you meet him, you'll know."

She leans over and gives me an awkward hug.

"Anyway," she says as she hops over to her bed. "*I* think you're pretty awesome, and mine is the only opinion that counts around here. Obviously."

"Thanks," I reply. "I think you're pretty awesome too."

"Of course I am."

A pause.

"Good night, Jennifer."

"Good night, Riley."

I close my eyes and block out the stars on the ceiling. In the shadows of my imagination, I let myself daydream about Branden smiling at me, taking my hand. Asking me on a date.

And I can almost let myself hope that in the real world, he'd mean it.

I wake up the next day with a strange mix of fear and excitement in my stomach. I'm up before the alarm—definitely a first for me—and jump on Riley's bed to wake her up.

"Riley! Riley!" I laugh. "It's Christmas!"

She groans and rolls over, burying her shock of hair beneath a pillow.

"No, it's not," she mumbles.

I pull the pillow off her. "Oh fine, you're right. But it *is* almost breakfast time, and I don't want to be late. Especially since we have warm-ups right after. I don't want to throw up all over Branden on our first day."

This makes Riley laugh, and she pushes herself up to sitting. "It would definitely make a lasting impression," she says. Then she pushes me to the side. "Okay, okay, let's go. But brush your teeth first—it smells like you ate cat poop in your sleep."

I laugh and make sure to breathe in her face before rolling off the bed and heading to the bathroom.

"How'd you sleep, ladies?" Tyler asks. We're all sitting at the same table in the corner; I keep hoping Branden will come sit by us, but no such luck. I spy him sitting with some of the guys from his hall, though he does glance over and catch my eye once.

"Like rocks," I say.

"Speak for yourself," Riley responds, picking at her eggs. "You snore."

I throw a balled-up napkin at her.

"Liar. I do not."

Riley looks at Tyler. "She does," she says. "And mumbles. I kept waiting for her to sing opera."

Tyler chuckles and runs a hand through his curly hair.

"Yeah, well, it can't be worse than my roommate. Stinky McStinkerson doesn't smell any better in the morning, let me tell you. *And* he snores like a train."

Riley laughs.

"Still not worse than Jennifer."

I shake my head. "You're horrible," I say.

"You love me."

"Speaking of," Tyler says, "when are you gonna make a move on that Branden kid?"

I stare at him, openmouthed, then glare at Riley. She tries to look innocent as she bites into her muffin.

"Oh, come on," Tyler says, "it's pretty obvious. I mean, you keep looking over at him."

"You're really bad at being discreet," Riley adds.

I shake my head.

"I'll make a move the same time you do," I say. I smile at Tyler, who raises an eyebrow. "I saw how you were staring at that acrobat."

"Kevin?" he asks. He breaks out into a grin. "Oh, sweetie, I've already made a move. We were chatting right up until sign-in last night. He's really cute, *and* he only lives twenty minutes away from me. Kind of perfect."

"Jealous," Riley says. "Gay boys always get the cute ones."

I elbow her. "You've got Sandy."

She nods. "Yes, but that's different. Besides, you're changing the subject. Tyler's brought his game, time for you to bring yours."

"Okay, okay," I say. "I'll talk to him at lunch."

"If not sooner," Tyler says with a wink to Riley.

"What's that supposed to mean?" I ask. But of course he won't tell me. He just goes back to eating his scrambled eggs.

• • •

Just my luck: I find out what Tyler meant on the *sooner* side.

A few minutes after breakfast, we all gather in the gymnasium for group warm-ups. According to the program, this will be a daily thing—another team-building activity to keep us all on the same page. Except today, rather than gathering with our practice groups after, we head straight into auditions.

We start with some simple cardio: We run a few laps around the gym, then do some jumping jacks. It just gets worse from there. After jumping jacks, we pair off into two lines and start doing what they call "floor work." Cartwheels (both sides), somersaults (front and back), and then these inchworm things that are more like moving push-ups.

Ten minutes in and I'm already sweating more than I ever have before; not even gym was this intense, and our gym teacher is known throughout the district as being one of the meanest there is. Mr. Jeffers has nothing on these circus coaches.

I stand beside Riley after we're done doing the inchworm things, trying not to look like I'm panting as hard as I really am. Riley looks a little winded, but nowhere near as bad as I am. When I look over to Tyler, I'm jealous to see he's barely broken a sweat. I do everything I can not to look at Branden—if I'm being that obvious to my friends, I can only hope he hasn't caught on as well.

Not that there's any time to worry about that. Right after we do the floor passes, Leena—who's taken charge of warm-ups this morning—calls out that it's time to partner up for some light conditioning. I glance at Riley. She winks at me. And then, before I can safely call her my warm-up partner, she skips off toward Tyler and takes him by the hand.

I glare at them.

But then there's a tap on my shoulder.

"Want to be partners?"

I look back and my heart skips a beat. Branden.

"Um, sure," I say.

"Cool."

He's in gym shorts and a tank top again, and he looks even more muscular up close. Like Tyler, he doesn't look like he's even winded after all the warm-ups. Riley gives me a little wave and wink as Branden guides me toward another side of the mat.

First conditioning activity? Sit-ups. Great. I don't think I've done a sit-up outside of gym class in months.

"Ladies first," he says.

"You're *such* a gentleman," I respond.

"I know." He grins. "How was the rest of your night?"

"It was all right," I say, lying down. "How about you? What was your prize?"

He laughs as he kneels on my feet. "Granola bars," he says. "And OJ. Super-awesome prize."

I want to make small talk, but then Leena blows her whistle and it's workout time. I cross my arms over my chest and start doing sit-ups. This is *not* how I'd hoped our first encounter was going to go. Here I am, sweating and trying my hardest not to grunt, and every time I sit up I'm greeted by Branden's brown eyes staring intently into mine. It's too much, too embarrassing, and I know the red on my cheeks isn't just from exertion. I squeeze my eyes shut and try to pretend I'm anywhere else, doing anything else. When the whistle finally blows again, I flop back on the mat and let out a huge sigh.

"Not bad," he says. He pats me on the knee. "You only looked like you were going to pass out for part of it."

"Thanks," I say. "I think."

Then we switch places. When Leena blows the whistle, I look everywhere but at Branden—otherwise I know I'll blush again. I spot Megan paired up with one of her sisters across the gym. When she catches my eye, she scowls.

For the first time in this entire warm-up, I smile.

Chapter ● Six

After a few more embarrassing partner exercises—the worst being a split stretch, where I learned Branden was actually a *lot* more flexible than me—we break off for auditions. It quickly became apparent during the warm-ups that that wouldn't be my big chance at impressing him. Which means my last and only hope is trying out for the flying trapeze. But first, I have to try out for a ground skill, which means Riley takes my arm at the end of warm-ups and drags me out of the gymnasium.

"I hate you," I say when Branden's out of earshot. He had told me he was trying out for the acro class. While he was doing push-ups, of course.

"No, you don't," Riley says.

I want to refute her, but it's not worth it. Because she did exactly what she said she would—she got me to talk to Branden before lunch. If only it had been more than a few sweaty snippets. We head out of the gym and to one of the small tents set up outside. It's still a little chilly, but the moment we step inside the red-and-yellow tent, goose bumps are the last thing on my mind. The early day sun makes the canvas glow, so the interior has a warm, unearthly sort of feel. And it smells like damp grass and vinyl, some strange mixture that immediately makes me think of all the shows I saw growing up. Today I'm actually a part of that history.

I know it's silly, but it's honestly like being onstage. There are juggling balls and pins and rings set up on a few tables in the center of the tent and a single row of bleachers along the side. So, yeah, no audience, but this is the first time I've stepped into a tent knowing that I was going to perform. Well, audition. But still, I'll be doing it in front of people.

"What did he say?" Riley whispers while we wait for the coaches to show. "Did he ask you out? Did you ask *him* out?"

"No," I say. I keep my voice down; even though none of the Twisted Triplets are here, I don't want this conversation getting back to them. Growing up in this town has taught me one thing: Gossip carries fast in small crowds. "It wasn't exactly good timing."

"Pansy," she responds. The coach entering the tent prevents me from responding.

The guy is in his late twenties, and he's got a huge handlebar mustache and goatee and paisley shirt. Definitely the juggling coach. The woman who comes in with him is a little more refined, with long hair in a ponytail and leggings under her short, flowery skirt.

"Hey, everyone," he says. "I'm Jim, and Hilary and I are the juggling coaches for this session." Hilary does a little curtsy. "We're actually going to do a mixture of floor work here, including rolling globe and rolla bolla, and we're not into the whole competing-for-a-spot thing. If you're here auditioning, you have a spot in the show." He looks around at the assembled kids—there are maybe ten of us in all, including Riley and me. "That said, we'd still love to see what you're bringing to the table. Who wants to show us what they've got?"

As expected, Riley's the first to raise her hand. She goes up while the rest of us take our spots on the bleachers. Once everyone's settled, she picks up six juggling balls and begins tossing them while doing a little dance. When she's done, everyone applauds, and she sits down beside me.

I wait until the very end to go up. At first I wasn't nervous, but then everyone else goes up and shows off tricks I couldn't even dream of doing, and I really wish I had just gone after Riley. I know Jim said that we didn't need to be experts already, but when I finally step up and grab three balls off the table, I wish I'd had more than a night's worth of practice. My hands are shaking; I hope no one notices.

"I'm Jennifer," I say, trying to focus equally on Jim, Hilary, and Riley, "and I'm . . . well, I'm actually entirely new to this. But Riley taught me the basics last night, and I'm hoping I can learn more while I'm here." I don't say that I'm only here because I'm terrified I won't be good at flying trapeze. I have a feeling that wouldn't leave a good first impression.

Much to my surprise, I don't mess up; I manage nine full tosses before I catch the last ball and set them down on the table.

"Very nice," Jim says as I sit down. "Especially for an absolute beginner."

He glances down at his watch.

"Well, it looks like we've got about twenty minutes before your next set of auditions, so if you'd like, we can just start in on a little lesson. I'm feeling pretty good about this group, aren't you, Hil?"

Hilary nods. "Definitely. I think we'll be able to do a lot with these guys. I'm already dreaming up some choreography."

Jim grins at her, then hops from the bleachers and has us gather around the table.

"Nice job," Riley whispers into my ear. I smile, suddenly realizing there's adrenaline pumping in my veins from putting on a show. It feels good. No, it feels *great*. And when Jim starts teaching us something called a "Mills Mess," I actually start to feel like I belong here.

When the lesson is done and I've almost mastered the trick, Riley and I part ways outside the tent.

"Good luck," she says.

"Thanks. What are you auditioning for now?"

She shrugs. "Nothing. I'm just focusing on juggling this time around. Maybe next year I'll try climbing things. I just don't have the upper body strength yet."

Neither do I, I want to say, but then I might talk myself out of auditioning. Riley heads back into the tent to chat with the coaches, leaving me to stare out across the field to the flying trapeze rig. My heart settles somewhere up in my throat as I watch two people—I'm guessing it's the coaches—swing back and forth on the trapeze. One lets go and latches onto the other's hands, then releases and does a somersault to the net below.

"You ready for this?" comes Branden's voice. I jump and look over to him.

"I . . . honestly, no." No point trying to play it cool—he already saw me sweating on my second push-up.

He pats me on the back. I can't help but wonder if his hand lingers there on purpose or by accident.

"I'm sure you'll be great," he says. "My first time was terrifying, but it's a rush. You'll be addicted in no time."

I try to smile, but I'm suddenly feeling nauseated as I watch another figure climb the ladder and then swing out over the net. Even from here it looks ridiculously high up.

"How was your juggling audition?" he asks.

"Great," I reply. "I got in. Well, everyone got in, but I managed not to screw up."

He chuckles.

"Better than me, then. I totally blew my floor routine. Managed to face-plant after a backflip."

"Are you okay?" I ask, glancing over to make sure there's no bruising. But no, he looks just as gorgeous as he did doing sit-ups this morning. People shouldn't be allowed to look pretty while working out.

"Yeah," he says. "Just hurt my pride."

We walk slowly toward the trapeze rig. Only a few other campers are heading that way, and right now we're pretty much alone on the field. Maybe it's the excitement from the audition, but being with just him doesn't make me nearly as nervous as it would have yesterday. Maybe Big Top Jennifer is starting to flourish.

"So do you think you'll get in?"

He shrugs. "I don't know. But it's only a week, so it won't hurt my feelings too much. I mainly just care about flying trap—it's impossible to find schools near here. I've had to drive out of state for most of my training."

"What's your dream?" I ask.

He pauses and looks at me. Crap, maybe that was too silly a question.

"My dream?"

"Yeah," I murmur, trying to save face. "What do you want to do with all this training?"

He smiles at me. "Ideally, join a circus. Find some super-attractive, talented trapeze partner to do some duo work with. But there aren't too many girls around here who do flying trapeze, either."

And there's no helping it this time. I really do blush.

"What about you?" he asks, as though he doesn't even notice the brilliant red flush to my cheeks. It feels like my face is on fire. "What brought you here?"

"I've always wanted to do it," I say for what feels like the hundredth time. "Maybe someday I'll be good enough to be part of a show. I mean, I'd love to be part of a show. Just have to survive that long, I guess."

"We all have to start somewhere," he says. He gives me a winning smile. I smile back. It's easy to be around him, easy to talk to him. I know it sounds stupid, but I feel like I've known him for more than a few hours.

"Speaking of," he says, glancing to the rig, which we've almost arrived at. "I think it's time to fly."

Chapter ● Seven

There are six other people trying out for flying trapeze, and there's only one other girl. A quick glance at them all confirms my worst fears: They've clearly done this before. Everyone is staring at the rig with that sort of look, like this is all routine and there's no worry they won't get in. I feel a light sheen of sweat break out on my skin. The rig is even taller up close, and the white rope net strung between the tall beams looks way too thin to actually support someone's weight. I step a little close to Branden, until our arms almost touch, and try not to faint.

There are four coaches here, and they introduce themselves as Michael, Tanya, Joe, and Marty. They're each in the green Karamazov Circus T-shirts, and they look like they work out all day, every day. I really, really should have tried some pull-ups before coming here.

"So," says Tanya, who is apparently in charge. She has long brown hair and is maybe five feet tall. I remember meeting her last night after sign-in, when she and Leena checked to make sure we were all accounted for. "Has everyone flown before?"

There's a general nodding of heads. Then I raise my hand tentatively and speak up.

"I haven't."

She clearly recognizes me, too, as her serious face breaks into a smile.

"Not a problem, Jennifer. Everyone's a beginner at some point. We'll just make sure you're in lines to start out with." She addresses the rest of the group. "We'll get you warmed up with a few simple swings—everyone in lines until we know your skill level. If you want to try going into splits or planche to start out, that's fine. We mainly want to make sure you have proper form—the tricks aren't so important right now." Then she steps up beside me. "I'll talk you through what they're doing," she says. "Watch closely. When it's your turn to fly, I'll shout out directions while you're in the air. It's easy, trust me." She puts her hand on my shoulder. "You've got this."

I don't know if I believe her.

Michael, the burlier of the coaches, walks over to a set of ropes hanging down from a pulley system strung between the two tall trapeze points. Joe and Marty help the rest of the kids into these wide belts covered in metal loops.

Joe scurries up the tiny rope ladder toward the platform at the top. Once he's there, Branden goes up and waits on the wooden plank—it looks so tiny from here, like it's only a few feet across. I nearly swoon, and I'm not sure if it's because I know I'm about to see Branden in action or if it's because I'm suddenly insanely worried he'll fall and break his neck. Branden's clearly not concerned, though; he stays still as Joe clips the other end of the ropes into Branden's belt loops. Right. Safety lines. Of course we'd be in safety lines.

See, Jennifer, you're perfectly safe. Nothing can go wrong.

But that's really hard to keep in mind when Branden grabs the trapeze and swings out over the net. He beats his legs back and forth, his whole body streamlined and straight and perfectly in unison with the swing of the trapeze. Tanya talks me through the entire thing, telling me about the proper body positions to get a swing going and keep it steady. She even has me try it out on the ground—she has me hold my hands over my head with my stomach tucked in and pelvis tilted up so my spine is perfectly straight, then has me bring my arms down to make a seven shape. I'm so wrapped up in trying to get the pose right that when I see Branden drop from the trapeze, I nearly scream.

He plummets to the net, face-first, hands at his sides. The net heaves when he hits, then he's propelled back up and does a flip in the air before landing again on his butt. My pulse races, proper form forgotten. But no one else is panicking, and when he lowers himself down from the edge of the net, there's a big grin on his face. Tanya chuckles when she sees my shocked expression.

"And that," she says, "is how you get down. It's very important you don't try to land on your hands and knees—the real risk in this isn't hitting your head, but getting your fingers or toes caught in the net. That's when things snap. Michael will watch the lines so you don't go too fast."

I suppress a shiver.

"So I just have to land face-first?"

"Yep." She pats me on the back. "It takes a while, but you'll get used to it."

Right.

I have a feeling that plummeting face-first toward the ground goes against every survival instinct I have. "Getting used to it" isn't exactly something I want to do. I like having survival instincts, thanks.

Branden walks over and hands me his belt. I blush as I take it and strap it onto my waist, making it tighter than is reasonably comfortable. He doesn't leave my side. There are still five others to go, and Tanya talks me through the key points of every swing—when to beat, when to assume what position, when to let go. By the time it's my turn, my heart is hammering a thousand times a second, and I'm pretty sure I won't even be able to hold on to the bar from all the sweat on my hands. But Branden smiles at me when Tanya tells me it's my turn to fly, and I try to force some confidence into my veins.

I can do this, I can do this, I can do this.

I walk over to the ladder, which is actually just two long ropes with a bunch of wooden bars strung between them. "Stable" is probably the last word I would use to describe it. I glance up at the platform. Vertigo makes my world spin. The platform is easily two stories high, if not taller, and I have to get there without being tied into safety lines. Joe motions for me to climb, and I try to imitate the way the others did it, one foot on either side of the ladder so it's like I'm climbing it sideways. The moment all my weight's on it, the ladder gives a sickening little twist.

I squeeze my eyes shut and take a long, deep breath. I'm not even a foot off the ground and I'm terrified, and what's worse, everyone is watching. I can practically feel Branden's stare burning into my back. What if I screw up? What if I let go when I'm not supposed to or miss the net entirely or . . . ?

No, this is your time to shine. So get up this ladder and shine!

I force my eyes open and take another breath. It does nothing to calm my frantic pulse or ease the shake in my hands, but I manage to release my death grip on the ladder and reach up for the next rung. The ladder sways again and then stops. Tanya's there at the base, holding it relatively steady.

"This is always the hardest part," she says quietly. "You can do this."

I nod. I climb.

Having her steady the base makes it a little easier, but when I'm about halfway up, the ladder gives another twist and I make a huge mistake.

I look down.

Two things go through my head in the very same instant.

The first is that I'm really high up, and the net, although directly beneath me, is so hard to see it looks like it isn't there. The second is that every single person around the rig is watching me. Waiting for me to mess up. Or fall. Or worse.

I freeze.

It's like my hands fill with concrete. I can't release my grip, can't force myself up another step. A breeze blows past, making the ladder sway a small amount, but it feels like being caught in a tornado. Once more, I squeeze my eyes shut. This time, though, I can't get the image of the ground from my head, nor can I push down the nausea rising in my throat. I'm going to vomit. I'm going to vomit halfway up a rope ladder, and there's nothing anyone can do to stop it. With my luck, I'll probably get it on Branden.

"You're almost there," Joe calls from up top. His voice seems so far away. I know he's not, I know it's only a few more climbs, but I also know I can't do it. I just can't. I'm going to fail at this like I've failed at dating and everything else. "Just a few more climbs and you're okay."

I shake my head.

No, I'm not okay. This is so far from okay it hurts. Branden is watching along with the rest of the camp and this is my first day and everyone is going to know that I'm a coward. But it's worse than that—much worse. I'll never be a trapeze star. All those years of hoping and dreaming have boiled down to this one moment. And I can't even climb the ladder.

All those hopes and dreams were for nothing.

I want the whole rig to fall into a hole and swallow me up. That doesn't happen, of course. No, it's worse than that: My grip starts to slip.

My hands shake and the sweat gets worse and I'm going to fall. I'm going to miss the net and fall to my death, and I'll forever be known as the girl who died trying to climb a rope ladder.

"Just come down," Tanya calls. I huddle closer to the ladder. My grip slips another millimeter. I can't come down. I can't move. I can't.

"Come on, Jennifer," she says. "You got this. Just come down and you can try again later on. You're totally okay."

I don't move. Not until I hear another voice. A voice I really, really wish wasn't nearby right now.

"You can do it, Jenn," Branden says. His words cut me to the bone.

In that moment, I want to be anywhere but there. Not even on the ladder—no, I mean I don't want to be at the camp. I don't want to be anywhere near the circus or all these people who know I was too scared to climb a ladder.

Maybe that's what forces me to move my hand, that desire to run away. But something fills me, and with one shaky movement after another, I make my way down the ladder, slowly but surely, keeping my eyes shut the entire time. Someone's hand is on my back when I get closer to the ground. Then my feet touch grass.

I open my eyes to see Tanya standing there, a comforting smile on her face, her hand still on my back, keeping me steady.

And beside her is Branden. He isn't smiling. He looks concerned.

"See?" Tanya begins.

Whatever she is about to say is lost to me, though. I can't stay there. I can't listen. Before she finishes her sentence, I run off, straight toward the dorm, and I don't stop for anyone. Especially not for Branden.

Chapter ✸ Eight

'm pretty certain I'll never step outside of this dorm room again. I'll wait until the camp is over, and then my mom and dad can come get me and drag me out, maybe with a blanket over my head so no one can see it's me. I huddle on my bed, back against the wall and the sheets tangled around me, and I wait. If I got out my phone now, could my parents be here before the rest of the troupe knows and I'm the laughingstock of the camp? The only plus side to this debacle is that I don't know anyone here from town. When break is over, I'll go back to being miserable little Jennifer Hayes, and no one will know that I failed so hard.

It's better if I don't think of how I'll answer my friends' questions: *How was it? Are you doing it again? Are you gonna run away to the circus now?*

I'm not good at lying, but after this I think I might have to learn.

There's a knock at the door a few minutes later, and I wonder if it's my parents, alerted that I'm a failure at circus and they need to take me home. It's definitely not Riley—she'd just barge in.

For some reason, I don't move from the bed or call out. The knock doesn't come again, so I figure they've moved on. But then the door opens, slowly, and Leena says my name.

"Yeah?" I respond. I pull the blankets tighter around me. Not that I'm cold—I'm still sweating from adrenaline—but I want to hide as much of me as I can.

Leena steps in. Her brown hair is in a braid, and she has cosmic-swirl leggings underneath her shorts. I wonder if they pulled her away from coaching the aerial hoop. I wonder if that means the whole company knows by now.

"Hey," she says. She says it in that voice grown-ups use, like they're talking to a caged animal or someone very stupid. "Are you okay? I heard what happened."

"I'm fine," I lie. *See, Jennifer? Not so hard after all.*

Sadly, Leena doesn't take the bait. She steps into the room and closes the door quietly behind her.

"Let me guess," she says, leaning against Riley's desk. "Vertigo, right?"

I don't say anything.

"Ugh, that's why I hate flying trapeze." She sighs. "You know, I've been doing this circus thing for ten years now and was a gymnast for ten years before that. And not once have I flown on a flying trapeze."

"Really?" I ask in spite of myself.

"Yeah," she says. She shrugs. "What can I say? I hate heights."

I can't help but laugh. "But you perform, like, every day. In the air."

"It's different," she says. "When I'm on the hoop, *I'm* in control. I'm not being swung about, and I don't dismount by landing on my face. Personally, I think they're crazy. But I guess we all are."

I don't say anything when she quiets down. After a few moments, she continues.

"When I first tried out for lyra, I was horrible. I'd done gymnastics for years, like I said, but the hoop was a whole different beast. I still remember, I was with the rest of my gymnastics team—we were doing a weekend intensive for fun. I was the first one to go up and try it out. And I managed to fall flat on my face."

"Ouch."

"Yeah, ouch."

I expect her to say, *But then I got right up there and tried again,* like all those uplifting stories my parents would try to tell me when I wasn't good the first time around. In other words, I expect her to be entirely unhelpful.

"My pride was hurt worse than my body. But you know what?" *Here it comes.* "I didn't get back on that thing the entire weekend we were there. I just watched from the sidelines and took down notes and figured out what my teammates were doing wrong. I thought about it every night before bed, going over moves and sequences. And then, about a month later, I went in for a private lesson. It was the first time I'd been on a hoop since I fell, and I figured I'd be scared out of my wits. But I got on the hoop, no problem, and was able to do everything I'd seen my teammates do, but without making the same mistakes they did. I never was the first to be good at something, but I was always the one who refused to give up. I'm pretty sure that's what made me stronger, and I know that's why Olga hired me onto her show. She knew I wouldn't give up, not when I was sick or tired or wanting to do something else. It was persistence, not sheer skill, that made me who I am today."

I can't help but look at her in a new light—I'd always seen her under the spotlights, always glittering and perfect. It's nearly impossible to imagine her as anything else.

"So . . . ," I begin.

"So, you shouldn't let this get you down. Maybe flying trapeze isn't your thing. Maybe it is. This week won't ruin your career, trust me. If you're really passionate about something, you'll do it. Girls like you and me don't give up so easily."

"Easy for you to say," I mutter. I don't want to be whiny, not in front of her, but I can't help it. "The whole camp knows I'm a coward by now. I'll be the joke for the rest of the week."

She shrugs. "Maybe," she says. I look at her—that wasn't the response I expected, but her honesty is, oddly, nice. If a little brutal. "I'm not going to pretend that word won't spread. But I think you'll be surprised—the kids who come to circus camp, well, they aren't your normal jocks or gossip queens. Not usually. In my experience, we were all outcasts in some way, which is why we turned to the circus to feel at home. Give these guys a chance; they might actually surprise you in their willingness to look past your shortcomings." She looks at me, considering. "That said, if by tomorrow you really want to leave, you're more than welcome to go. We'll even refund part of your tuition in hopes you try again next year. No one will hold it against you."

She pauses to let what she said sink in.

"Lunch is in twenty minutes. The casting announcements will be posted near the end, so I'd recommend you try to make it. And by that, I mean you're obligated to go to lunch." She winks. "Can't have you skipping out on meals—you need your strength."

"What's the point?" I ask, once again failing at the whole not-whining thing. "It's not like I made it into flying trapeze."

"You never know," she says. "And there are plenty more skills to learn under the big top. Don't discount them all just yet."

She pushes herself from the desk.

"I'll let you be. No doubt Riley will be back here soon to check on you. Do you need anything before I go?"

I shake my head.

"Okay then. Well, I'll see you at lunch."

Then she opens the door and steps out into the hall, leaving me with the empty room and the fragile hope that maybe the door hasn't closed on my circus career just yet.

• • •

Leena was right about one thing. Not even two minutes have passed when Riley comes in, opening the door tentatively like it might set off a bomb. I wonder if she passed Leena on her way here.

"Jennifer?" she asks, peering around the edge of the door.

"Yeah," I say, and she walks in. A small part of me is ashamed that Riley's treating this like she's intruding on my space when it's her room as well. For some reason, it also makes me a little upset; I don't want her to think she has to baby me. "It's okay, I'm not going to snap at you."

"Oh, I don't care about that," Riley says, sitting down on her bed. "I just didn't know if you were still throwing up all over the place."

"I didn't throw up at all," I say. *I wanted to, but I didn't.*

"Yeah, I figured as much. Megan was telling everyone you got really sick on the trapeze. And I mean, *really* sick, like projectile-vomiting-across-the-field sick."

I sit up a little straighter and push the blankets off me. Of course Megan was spreading rumors.

"She wasn't even there," I say.

"Don't worry, no one else believes her either."

"Why would she say that?" I ask, even though I know precisely why. For some reason, that girl has it in for me.

Riley shrugs. "Jealousy is an ugly monster," she says. Then she looks at me, a little more serious. "How *are* you doing, anyway? Do you need anything?"

I shake my head. "I just froze. I'm not sick or anything."

She nods. "Well, the offer still stands. Even if it means you need me to kick Megan's blond butt."

I laugh, which admittedly feels strange; I didn't think I'd have the capacity for that anymore today.

"Thanks," I say.

"That's what friends are for—petty revenge." She smiles, hops off her bed, and tries to pull me off mine. "Anyway, I'm glad you don't need anything, because I actually just came here to drag you off to lunch."

I put up resistance, but that eyebrow raise of her speaks volumes.

"Never get in between me and my food," she says gravely. "Sandy learned that one the hard way. At least, that's how I explained those hickeys to his parents." To accentuate the point, she leans over and nibbles on my arm, making loud gnawing sounds.

I giggle and let her pull me off the bed.

"Okay, okay! I give. I need that arm."

Riley stands straighter and smiles, then takes me by the arm and skips me out the door.

Chapter ● Nine

Okay, I hadn't honestly expected the entire lunchroom to stop talking and stare at me when I walked in, but the nagging fear was there as Riley half guided, half dragged me toward the cafeteria. So the fact that I'm able to not only walk in, but get my food and sit at a table without anyone so much as looking at me twice, kind of blows my mind. If this was high school, there'd be at least one group of girls snickering behind my back.

That said, I don't even bother trying to find Megan and her sisters in the crowd—I've no doubt that they're definitely talking about me. Maybe they're still trying to spread the rumor that I threw up all over the trapeze rig. Having Riley at my side honestly makes me not care so much.

Riley and I sit next to Tyler and a couple of his acro buddies.

They all give the cursory hello and then go back to chatting about the tricks they nailed or screwed up during auditions.

"I heard what happened," Tyler says to me, keeping his voice low. "You okay?"

"I didn't throw up."

"Shame," he says with a wicked smile. "It would have made such a good story. So what happened? Vertigo?"

I nod. "Turns out I don't like heights."

"Join the club," Riley says around a mouthful of her burger.

"You are just the portrait of a lady," Tyler says, staring at her.

She grins and lets a few crumbs drop from her mouth. "Yep!" she says happily.

Tyler shakes his head in mock disgust, then turns back to me. "Well, don't worry about it. So long as you stay around this one, you'll always appear to have more social grace."

"I'm going to pretend I don't know what that means," Riley says.

"Please do. And chew with your mouth closed."

In response, Riley makes her gnawing noise again and buries her face in the burger.

I laugh, then look across the cafeteria and spot Branden. My humor dies in my chest; he's sitting beside Megan, her other sisters nearly blocking him from my view.

"What is she doing with him?" I say, not meaning to utter it aloud.

Tyler follows my stare.

"Don't worry," he says. "She doesn't stand a chance."

But there's a sick feeling in my gut as I watch them talk. He laughs at something she says, and I don't miss the way her hand brushes against his as she reaches for a napkin. Suddenly all I can think of is Josh, the guy who stood me up, and the way he went for a cheerleader not a week after tormenting me.

"You're totally not listening, are you?" Tyler asks, nudging me with his elbow.

I jerk and look back at him. Was I really just staring at Branden like a lovesick idiot?

"Sorry," I say. Because he's right, I didn't hear anything.

He sighs.

"I said, *how was juggling?*" He asks the question unnecessarily slowly.

"Good," I respond.

"Really good," Riley says, wiping her mouth with a handful of napkins. "Jennifer's picking it up real quick. I spoke with Jim after the audition, and I think we're going to try to set up a partner routine."

I look at her, surprised.

"What?" she asks. "I told him I wanted to work with you, and he agreed. So yeah. You're definitely in." She wraps an arm across my shoulders. "And you're stuck with meeee!" she sings.

"I feel so sorry for you," Tyler says.

"Could be worse," I say. "I could be stuck in contortion with those three."

Riley snorts with laughter.

"That would definitely be a worse fate."

"What about you?" I ask Tyler. "What did you audition for?"

"Acro and rope," he says. "Though I spoke with one of the coaches who works as a hand balancer professionally. I guess they don't technically teach it during the camp, but he offered to train me on the side. Your boy Branden was there as well, auditioning for Cyr wheel. He's good. Really good. Except at backflips—kid nearly broke his own nose. Too bad he plays for your team."

"I thought you had your eyes set on the acro boy. Kevin?" Riley asks.

"Oh, I do," he says. He grins at Kevin, who catches Tyler's gaze, returns it, then blushes and goes back to talking with a couple of the girls from my hall. "But that doesn't mean I can't admire beauty. And Branden is pretty beautiful."

I sigh without meaning to and catch myself staring again at Branden, who's still sitting with Megan and her sisters. Branden, who looks so much more at home surrounded by that much talent and beauty. Tyler says Megan doesn't stand a chance, but I think he's just trying to make me feel better. Branden's cut out to be with someone immensely talented. I've already proven that's not me.

After that realization, it's practically impossible to find my appetite. I pick at the fries on my plate and listen to everyone else talking around me. But I'm already drifting. They're already moving faster than I ever will.

• • •

Near the end of lunch, right after they bring out a tray of what I thought were brownies but are actually chocolate-chip granola bars—a terrible misconception, albeit still tasty—Olga nonchalantly walks over to a bulletin board on the wall and pins up three sheets of paper. The casting announcements. She's barely taken a step to the side before half the camp is jumping from their chairs to see them. I'm not among the first, that's for sure; I already know I'm not getting into flying trapeze.

Still, when I do make it up there, I'm a little disappointed to see that I was right. Riley stands at my side and congratulates me on getting into juggling with her, even though that was kind of a giveaway. I feel a little sick to see I was the only one who auditioned who didn't get into flying trapeze. Branden's name is at the top, a reminder that he and I are on completely different social levels. And seeing as how we won't have any training together, I might as well get used to that fact now.

"Such a shame," comes a voice beside me. The drawl makes my skin crawl. "Here I was hoping we'd get to see more of your amazing aerial acrobatics."

I glare at Megan, who is staring at the announcements with a contented, malicious smile on her face, like a cat who just ate a large and tasty mouse. Every part of me wishes I had some sort of snappy comeback, but I've got nothing. Not that I have any time to respond. She looks at me, her grin widening.

"It's probably for the best. Can't have you thinking you're good enough for Branden, can we?" Then she winks and spins on her heel, walking off toward the exit, where the rest of her sisters are waiting.

"I really, really hate her," I mutter.

"I think the feeling's mutual," Riley replies. I nearly jump—I'd forgotten she was even standing there. Just shows how much Megan gets to me, seeing as Riley's hair makes her stand out in a crowd. I look around the cafeteria but Branden's already gone, probably off to afternoon practice. "Come on," Riley says, once more taking me by the arm. "Juggling will help. And if you're really frustrated, we can just start throwing clubs at each other. That's always helped me de-stress."

Chapter ● Ten

The rest of the afternoon passes in a fairly contented blur. It's hard to focus on not getting into flying trapeze when there are juggling pins being hurled at my head. Riley's decided she and I are going to do a partner act for the final show. But she wasn't happy with just a normal ground routine, no. She wanted to add "an extra level of danger."

Which, to her, meant doing the entire routine on top of rolling globes, which are exactly what they sound like—giant plastic balls I'm somehow supposed to balance on while throwing pins. Our coaches taught us how to stand and even walk a little bit, and although I only fell off a few times, I have a feeling it's going to be nearly impossible to combine it with juggling. Still, Riley is relentless with her optimism, and when the first session of practice is over four hours later, she's already discussing our music choices as we wander over to dinner.

We pass by one of the smaller circus tents—the blue-and-gold one—and Tyler steps out with a couple of other acro kids. He's covered in sweat and chatting animatedly with Kevin. When they walk, the backs of their hands brush.

"Hey, boys," Riley says, jumping over to walk beside Tyler. "How was practice?"

"Awesome," Tyler says. "I made it to nine chairs."

"It was really impressive," Kevin replies.

The four of us head to the dining room together. We don't talk about TV shows or video games, not like my other friends. No, the entire way there we talk about practice and how sore we are and what we're envisioning our routines will look like. Even though I've only been doing this a day, it's easy to get swept up in it, to start dreaming of my life under the circus lights—albeit in a different act. I won't lie, though—even with Riley's excitement, I'm still a little ashamed I won't be making my big debut on the trapeze rig. It's one of those things I try not to think about, otherwise I just get sad. So I let myself fall into Riley's dream of a fantastic partner act and try to mimic her enthusiasm.

When we get to dinner, however, the exhilaration of practice quickly plummets. Branden is standing in line for food, and Megan's right beside him, one arm looped through his like Riley's doing with me. Only their pose is definitely *not* in friendship. Megan is leaning into Branden and giggling about something that's probably stupid. He doesn't really react, but he isn't pushing her away, either.

I stop dead. I can't help it.

"Crap," Riley says, catching my glance. She takes a steady breath and looks at me. "Okay, maybe he *was* playing you."

"What a jerk," Tyler says.

"What's going on?" Kevin asks, looking between us and Branden. I shake my head.

"It's nothing," I respond. "It was never anything."

Then, before anyone can ask if I'm okay for the hundredth time today, I step forward into the dinner line and do my best to firmly push Branden and his new girlfriend from my mind.

Tyler and Kevin sit with us at dinner, and my friends fill Kevin in on everything that's happened—or, in this case, that hasn't happened—between Branden and me. For my part, I sit facing away from Megan and her new catch and try to ignore everything but my quinoa bake and sautéed greens. Branden is currently the last topic I want to be discussing. Mainly because I want to run over there and scream in his face for toying with me like that.

"What do you think the game will be tonight?" Tyler asks.

"No clue," I say. "But I'm hoping it doesn't involve dress-up."

"Oh, come on, you looked so cute as a fairy."

"I don't care what it is so long as we don't have to run," Kevin admits. "Seriously, I don't think I've worked out this much all year."

"This is just day one," Tyler says. "If you think it hurts now . . ."

"Easy for you to say," Kevin retorts. "You were doing handstands all afternoon. So I'm going to cross my fingers for dodgeball."

"Or tennis," Riley adds.

"Or arm wrestling," I say.

"I hate you," Tyler says. "All of you. But especially the redhead."

"Hey!" Riley and Kevin say at the exact same time. We all burst into laughter.

It turns out that none of our guesses are correct. Thankfully, the night's game doesn't actually involve running, either, so Kevin did partially get his wish. About half an hour after dinner, we all gather back in the gymnasium for the night's game. The lights are low and the radio's playing again. We all settle along the same wall; there are tables set up in the opposite corner, each one covered in a blanket hiding a lumpy mass. A few counselors are wandering back and forth over there, talking to themselves and holding up the blankets to one another so only they can see what's underneath.

"What do you think it is?" Riley whispers.

"I almost don't want to know," I reply.

The lights go up the moment Olga walks in. Once she appears, everyone goes quiet—we're all waiting for her announcement.

"Good evening, campers!" she says, smiling warmly. "I hope you all had a great first day. I've spoken with the coaches, and they agree that each and every one of you has brought a great deal of talent on board. We're already very excited for the final show, and we know you are as well! But we don't want to get too ahead of ourselves, now do we?

"Tonight's game is to help us prepare for the show. You're already doing so much to enhance your skills, so now we want to focus on a very important aspect of circus: stage presence. It's not enough to be good at an act. You have to be able to perform. And often, that involves a lot of improvisation and a strong rapport with your fellow cast members. Obviously, we can't just teach you to do this—you have to practice and discover the spark within yourself. To that end, allow us to introduce tonight's game: Improv Superstar!"

Epic music blares through the speakers. When it's done, Olga continues.

"You will be broken up into four teams at random. Each of you will then pick a table. Under each sheet is a set of props that you will need to integrate into a series of improv skits. Your fellow troupers and coaches will be the judges. And as usual, the winning team will get a special surprise."

"It better not be more granola," Tyler whispers in my ear.

One of the coaches comes around the group with a top hat then, and we each draw out a slip of paper with a letter on it. I pull an *A*, and am more than a little disappointed to realize that I'm the only one in our group to get it. Riley and Kevin both got *B*, and Tyler pulled *C*.

There's no time to get sentimental; we break up into our teams almost immediately. I head over to the juggling coach, Jim, who holds a large sign with A over his head. And then I get my next unfortunate surprise that night: Megan is on my team. At least she doesn't look happy about this either.

"Hey, guys," Jim says, "looks like we have a strong team here."

And I suppose he's right—we have three of the kids who I know auditioned as clowns, so comedy should be pretty easy for them. They'll make up for my lack of funny. Unless I have to do a skit with Megan. If I get to make fun of her, I'll have a field day. And I know I'd get points from Riley and Tyler, at the very least.

Jim goes over some basics of improv: Always say yes; if repeating something, use the rule of three; and never turn your back on the audience, unless it's entirely necessary and intentional.

"The important thing is to have fun. Chances are, if you're having fun, so is the audience."

"Actually," Megan whispers beside me, "the important thing is not to choke. Think you can handle that, Jennifer? Or should I keep a bucket handy?"

I bite my tongue and glare down at her—I don't feel I have much to use against this girl, so my height is my only resort. There's no point getting in a fight now. She's not worth it. It's like dealing with Internet trolls: If you say nothing, they fade away. And I really, really want this one to fade away. Or fall flat on her face. I'm not above taking the low road from time to time. Well, hoping for it, at least. I just wish I could figure out why she hates me. If I'm not a threat, why am I even on her radar?

Thankfully for her, there's no time for me to retort or for her to make another jab. Olga announces it's time to begin, and as a team, we run toward our table and get a look at our props.

I have no idea where they assembled all these things, but I have a solid suspicion that most of them are on loan from the clowns. I'm also really eager to see what the other teams got.

Our table is laden with odd props. There's a gramophone speaker that's painted pink and orange, dozens of silly-shaped sunglasses, tubes of foam and clown noses and a plate of silver spoons. And that's just on one corner of the table. There are also fake flowers and oversize watches and juggling pins and more. It's like some crazy clown aunt emptied her attic and left us with the bits she couldn't send to a thrift store. I stand there and stare down at it all and can't even begin to imagine how to use any of it in a skit.

Thankfully, Olga isn't just abandoning us.

"Okay, troupers!" she calls over the din of excited chatter, "your first skit is in thirty seconds. You'll need at least four team members, and the theme is 'awkward bus ride.'"

She's not even done speaking before Andy—one of the clowns—takes control and starts handing out props. He thrusts the gramophone speaker into my hands and asks, "How is your singing?"

"Not bad, I guess."

"Excellent," he says. "Just keep singing as loud as you can and play along!"

Thirty seconds later Olga calls the first team forward—of course, *A* goes first—and we assemble in the middle of the gym, right under the spotlights. I can feel the rest of the troupe watching us—watching *me*—and a cold sweat breaks out on my skin. I sense

Megan's glare in particular; she wasn't cast in this skit, so I imagine her there, in the shadows, throwing mental daggers at my back.

The four of us sit down on the floor in three rows—me all alone at the back, Andy at the front, and two others wearing giant hats and sunglasses in the middle. Andy nods to me, and I start to sing. Very off-key. And very loudly.

"Excuse me, ma'am," one of the middle kids says, "could you please turn that down?"

"Of course, dear," I say, and start singing louder.

Andy stops the imaginary bus and comes back to try to get me to quiet down, and there's a moment where he tries to pull the gramophone from my hands and falls on top of the other passengers. Much to my surprise, the audience starts laughing.

The skit lasts about a minute, maybe less—it's really hard to tell when you're acting—and by the end, everyone on the bus is singing along to my terrible song. Andy yells out, "Scene!" and we stand and do a quick bow.

"That was great," he tells me as we rush offstage. I just smile, suddenly very grateful I didn't leave that afternoon.

Chapter ✎ Eleven

Riley and Kevin's team goes next. Kevin and three other guys I've never met before go onstage for this one, and their bus ride skit involves Kevin getting soaked with a lot of water. I can't say I understand much of it, but it's still fun to watch. I glance over to Riley while the show is happening and know she wishes she were out there—she'd probably make the whole thing much funnier. She's good like that.

Next up is Tyler's team, and there's a small kick to my stomach when he and Branden step out into the spotlight. Try as I might, I can't even focus on the other performers—my eyes are glued to Branden, and I can't tell if the queasy feeling in my gut is anger or desire. The only consolation is the fact that every once in a while, I catch Tyler throwing Branden a small death glare. Knowing that Tyler's definitely still on my team makes me feel much better. If only I could get over my attraction to Branden.

Their skit starts with one of the kids running up like she's about to miss the bus. She's wearing a huge patchwork coat and a hat that I think is actually a felt flowerpot. She gratefully gets on board and squeezes herself in between Tyler and Branden, then begins removing things from her pockets and asking the boys to hold them.

It turns out that's the gist of the act; she pulls something out, like a rubber centipede, hands it to one of the boys, and they react. Usually by throwing it out the window. The scene ends when she pulls out a baby doll and the bus driver yells that they have a strict no-baby-flinging policy.

I roll my eyes at the bad acting, but if I'm being honest, that's not what I was focusing on. I couldn't take my eyes off Branden. I tried. I really tried to keep my attention glued to Tyler and his awkward acting, but my eyes kept sliding over to Branden.

Why did you pick her? I want to ask him. *Why wasn't I good enough for you?*

Then I catch Megan from the corner of my eye and those questions die on the floor. A part of me wants to fight for him, to try and show off and catch his attention and hold it. But then I remember—there are only a few days left, and then I'll probably never see him again. Even if he is from the next town over. I just have to make it through the next week without getting my heart broken and I'll be okay.

Shouldn't be too hard, right?

The next group goes on, and I see Branden glancing at me from the corner of his eye as he leaves the stage. My heart flips.

Okay, maybe this *will* be more difficult than I thought. Here's hoping practice will keep me busy.

The rest of the improv show picks up steam, and by the end I'm nearly in tears with laughter. It was so fun to watch that I don't even care that my team didn't win—that honor goes to Branden and Tyler's team. I wander over to Tyler to say good night and congratulate him. Branden stops me before I make it over.

"Jennifer," he says. The way he voices it, it sounds like a question and a concern.

"Yeah?"

It's nearly impossible to keep my pulse steady, but I think I'm moderately successful. At least until he puts his hand on my shoulder. Then my heart goes into overdrive.

"Are you okay?" he asks.

I catch Tyler's questioning look and shrug off Branden's hand. "Yeah, fine. Thanks."

"Can I talk to you?" he asks, but then Tyler steps up behind him and interrupts with a big hello and a huge hug.

"I can punch him if you want," Tyler whispers in my ear. I shake my head slightly, and then he steps back. "You looked good up there," he says, slapping Branden on the chest. "Wasn't she funny?"

"Yeah," Branden replies.

And then Megan steps up beside me like she's part of the gang.

"Hilarious," she says. She glances at me. "I'm so glad she's finding her place in the troupe. Every good show needs a joke."

"Hey," Tyler begins, taking a half step toward her. I grab his arm and pull him back.

"Come on," I say. "She's not worth it." And I drag Tyler back to the dorms.

"I don't understand her problem," Riley says, tossing a juggling ball back and forth between her palms. We're in the back stairwell, her and Tyler and I, and there's maybe twenty minutes until sign-in.

"Apparently Jennifer's her problem," Tyler says. "The way she was looking at you . . . Man, I'm surprised you made it out of there alive."

"She must see you as a threat," Riley responds. She tosses the ball to me; I barely catch it and nearly fall off the step when I do.

I laugh. "Clearly. I'm a huge threat."

"Territorial behavior," Tyler says. He snatches the ball from my hands and tosses it to Riley. "I hear girls are all about that sort of thing."

"Oh, please," Riley says. "Gay boys are worse."

Tyler just chuckles. "Maybe." He glances at me, then Riley. "So, are we still a 'Go' on Operation Brannifer?"

"Brannifer?" I ask.

Riley smiles and tosses me the ball; I'm expecting it this time, and the catch isn't nearly as sloppy.

"Code name. You know, Branden and Jennifer, sort of like Brangelina . . ."

"I got it," I say, tossing the ball back to her. "Do I even want to know?"

"Probably not," she replies. She turns her attention back to Tyler and tosses him the ball. "But I don't know. He doesn't seem to know what he wants, and I can't stand indecisive guys. I think she could do better."

"Maybe," Tyler says, "but I mean, this is her first kiss we're talking about. I personally think it should happen at the circus. So romantic."

Indignation flares for a hot second.

"You told him?" I ask.

Riley shrugs. "He guessed."

"She didn't even confirm it," Tyler says, tossing me the ball. "Which is how I knew it was true. Don't worry, your secret's safe. But I do still think you should go for it. I mean, Megan's clearly intimidated, which means you probably have a chance. You do still like him, don't you?"

Riley answers before I can. "Of course she doesn't. She would never like a guy who's all hot and cold."

I sigh and lean back against the steps, tossing the ball between my hands.

"To be honest, I do still like him. I just wish he'd man up and tell me if he liked me."

"Good luck, *amiga*," Tyler says. "In my experience, boys are horrible at expressing their feelings—gay *or* straight."

Riley nods gravely.

"If you want him, you're probably going to have to go for him yourself."

"I dunno," I say. "Do you think he's worth it?"

"If he's into you," Tyler says, "yeah. He's kind of the whole package."

"*If* he's not playing you like a jerk."

"There's really only one way to find out," Tyler continues.

"What's that?" I ask.

"You ask him to the dance."

The dance. I'd done my best to forget—dances and I never got along. The last time I went to a dance was in middle school, for homecoming, and it was only fun because the girls I went with decided to bail early. We spent most of the night eating ice cream and watching stupid horror movies. In our dresses, of course.

"Isn't it supposed to be the other way around? Shouldn't he be asking me?" I ask.

"Times change," Tyler replies. "I already asked Kevin." He grins wide. "He said yes, by the way."

Riley squeals "Cute!" and gives him a hug. "You two are adorable. I hope you get married and have adorable circus babies."

Tyler just laughs and tries to push her off him.

"Calm down, crazy lady," he says between gasps of laughter. "Remember, it's Brannifer we're focusing on now!"

"Right," Riley says. She lets go, and they both turn to me. "So."

"So?"

"How do we get Megan out of the picture and you into his muscular arms?" Riley can't even finish her own sentence without giggling.

I toss the ball at her gently, and she catches it before it reaches her face.

"I hate you both," I say. As expected, this just makes them giggle even harder.

Riley and I chat for a good two hours after sign-in. We're supposed to be asleep, but it's hard to close your eyes when your best friend won't stop talking about circus boys being the best and how our partner act is going to blow everyone in the audience away. She's convinced I'll be able to do all the advanced tricks with only three days of practice. I'm not so sure.

"Trust me," she says, turning out the light, "by the time our act is done, Branden will be head over heels in love with you."

I don't think I believe her. No offense to Riley, but I'm still not exactly . . . well, *proud* to be a juggler. I'm in the act because I failed at something else. How am I supposed to be excited? Or feel like I'm showing off? The one thing I wanted to do more than anything else was a bust. And I have a funny feeling that no matter how good the partner act is, it won't be good enough to impress Branden. He's already seen me at my worst.

"Isn't that a little weird?" I ask. "I mean, trying to impress him like that? Shouldn't you be telling me that he'll like me no matter what?"

"Meh," Riley says. "Showing off is natural. The animal kingdom does it all the time. And who are we, if not glorified, awkward animals?"

I don't try to argue the point. I pull the covers up around me and close my eyes. In less than twelve hours I've frozen on a trapeze, discovered my true friends, and realized the guy I like may or may not be interested in someone else. I can only hope that the rest of the camp is a little less chaotic. But, given the circumstances, I have a feeling that my life under the big top is just going to get a heck of a lot stranger.

Chapter ● Twelve

'm not usually a morning person, and I'm definitely not the type of girl who wakes up before her alarm with a smile on her face. But for some reason, when the alarm goes off and my dreams slide from memory, it feels like I'm being given a fresh start. It's my second full day of camp, and today there are no scary auditions, no awkward getting-to-know-you games. I have a friend group and an act in the works. I also have a boy's heart to win. I take a deep breath and roll over in bed, looking to Riley, who's managing to sleep through her phone's alarm ringtone. All that's sticking out of the tangled covers is her hair. I toss my pillow at her and grin when she jumps and mumbles herself awake.

"Wakey, wakey, eggs and bakey!" I call out.

She mumbles again and looks over at me.

"You're cruel," she says, her voice muffled from under the covers.

"Just repaying the kindness," I say. "Can't have my amazing juggling partner sleeping through breakfast." I throw my last pillow at her. She snatches it from the air with catlike reflexes.

"This is war," she mutters, covering her head with the pillow.

"Then all is fair," I say, and hop off the bed to head to the shower.

We spot Tyler and Kevin at breakfast and sit down across from them. I don't miss the quick motion when we approach—they were holding hands and quickly let go to eat their scrambled eggs. I catch Riley's eye and grin. Those two are already so cute together, it's almost not fair.

"Morning, ladies," Tyler says when we set our trays down.

"Morning, beautiful," Riley says to Kevin. She smiles when she sits. "Oh, and hello, Tyler."

Tyler laughs and rolls his eyes. "Charming as ever."

"What's the agenda for today?" I ask. I've already read the schedule, but who knows: They might have announced something new before we got to the cafeteria.

"The usual," Tyler replies. "Group warm-up, then practice, practice, practice."

"Any clue what we're doing tonight?" Riley asks.

"Talent show," Kevin says. He points to a sign on the wall. "Sign-ups are over there. Not mandatory, of course, but 'highly recommended.'"

"Great," I mutter. One more chance to show everyone just how little talent I actually have. If only I had some skill I could whip out and impress Branden with. Anything to make me a little more flashy than his contortionist crush.

Almost out of habit, I glance over to where Branden's sitting. Then I'm reminded why I shouldn't have bothered looking; he's sitting right next to Megan, her sisters on the other side. One of the sisters—I think it's Sara—notices my glance and gives me what actually looks like a weary gaze, like she's empathizing with my abject hatred at seeing Megan and Branden together. Which is stupid, because she's Megan's sister, so obviously Sara's on her side.

"She'll never give up, will she?" Riley asks, noticing my gaze.

"Doubtful," I say. "She's going in for the kill."

"That's okay," she says, nudging me. "Because neither will you. True love will win out!"

I tear my gaze away from Branden and look back to her. "True love?"

She smiles and shrugs. "Dream big."

"You should do something for the show," Tyler says. "You know, show her up."

I laugh. "Like what? I can't even do the splits."

"Group act," Tyler says. He looks to Riley. "I'm sure we can think of something impressive by tonight."

She mimes putting on a hat. "Thinking caps on, Watson."

"Sherlock never said that," Kevin says.

"I'm an artist. I'm allowed to improvise."

• • •

Riley and I team up for the morning warm-up because, apparently, the way to winning Branden's heart is now to play hard to get. When he steps into the gym with Megan attached to his arm like a leech, however, my heart sinks. Maybe playing hard to get is doing her a favor. Clearly, she's not using the same tactic, and her direct approach is definitely doing more than any of my coyness ever could.

Just seeing her touching his arm sends an equal mix of rage and jealousy flooding through my veins. I would do anything to trade places with her. I know Riley said he wasn't the type to play me, and I don't think he is. So why is he with her? Why isn't he trying to spend more time with me? Did the trapeze thing really bother him more than he let on?

Maybe if he asks me to the dance, I'll know for sure. I just hope I don't have to ask him first.

Riley snaps her fingers in front of my face. "Earth to Jennifer," she says, bouncing on her heels. I shake my head clear and look at her. "You're starting to stare."

"Really?" I ask.

"Yeah."

Luckily, I'm not given much more time to make a fool of myself. One of the coaches blows a whistle and the warm-ups begin, first with a few laps around the gym, then jumping jacks, and then some impromptu dancing to "loosen up those joints and get your creative juices flowing." I don't know if it achieves the latter, but it definitely makes me feel silly, and entirely unprepared for the actual dance coming up. These circus people know how to *move*.

After the dancing, we do partner crunches and push-ups, along with some evil thing called "hollow body" that involves lying with my back flat on the ground and my legs hovering inches from the floor. After about ten minutes of sweating through the workout, it's time for some stretching. In the back of my mind, I can't help but wonder how this is important to juggling, but at least everyone's doing the same work.

I thought seeing Branden and Megan together at breakfast was bad enough. I was wrong. Seeing them do partner stretches together, well, that's a whole new level of awkward. Megan's extreme flexibility just makes it worse.

"Ignore her," Riley says. She's leaning against my back, pressing my nose just a little bit closer to my knees as I reach for my toes. It's easy to follow her advice—it feels like my legs are on fire. In a good way. If it weren't for the fact that Megan situated herself and Branden practically right across from us, I would have completely forgotten she was there in light of the pain.

"I'm doing my best," I say, and bury my face back in my knees. Well, I attempt to, anyway.

I almost succeed, too, until we go into a straddle stretch. I actually blush when I look over and see Megan with her legs spread wide and her chest flat on the ground, Branden practically standing on top of her. Her eyes are closed, but he blinks his open and notices my quick stare. He gives me a look that's impossible to decode. If I didn't know better, I'd almost say he looks a little embarrassed.

I avert my eyes and focus on the stretch. I'm nowhere near getting my chest to the floor, but it still burns.

"More," I tell Riley, and she presses me even farther past the edge of comfort.

Riley and I head straight to the little tent outside the gym once warm-ups are over. As we pass Branden and Megan, Riley makes sure to exclaim, very loudly, "I'm so excited for our act tonight, Jenn! You're going to be amazing."

I don't know if it does anything beyond make me blush—those two might not have even heard it. I try not to let myself look at Branden again. *Hard to get, hard to get.* So I smile and laugh and say I can't wait either. I just hope I'm half as convincing as Riley. I also hope we're able to follow through with an act that isn't a complete disaster.

"What are we going to do?" I ask her once we're safely out of the gym and away from Branden and his contortionist "friend."

She shakes her head. "I was just about to ask you the same thing." She gives me a quick glance. "I'm just assuming you don't have some magical ground act you haven't told us about yet, do you?"

"Nope," I say with a shrug. "I already told you—this is the only circus I've done."

"What about something else? Something not circus? Like, if this was just a normal school talent show, what would you do?"

"Watch."

She nudges me in the ribs. It's a beautiful, sunny day outside, but

I don't feel the sunny optimism. I was so excited this morning. Funny how seeing Branden stretching with someone else was enough to pop that bubble. If only because I really wish that she had been *me*.

"Seriously," she says. "You have to have something up your sleeve. You're too cool to be boring."

I laugh. No one's actually called me cool before. At least, no one outside of my tiny circle of friends. Seeing as our usual pastime is playing video games together, that's not really saying much.

"Well," I say, "I was in our school musical last year."

Riley practically squeaks with excitement. She stalls outside the flap of the tent and grabs my arm.

"No way, really? You can sing and dance and all that?"

"Um, yes? I mean, I can sing. Sort of. I'm not so certain now that you're staring at me like that."

She smiles and hops up and down a few times.

"We could totally do a group musical number. I'm positive the boys would be down. You can sing and we'll be the backup dancers!"

"I don't know . . . ," I begin, but she cuts me off with a hug.

"Oh, this is going to be amazing! We're totally gonna blow that contortionist jerk out of the water."

And just like that, I've pretty much sealed my death warrant. There's no time to argue, either; Riley grabs my arm and drags me into the practice tent, already rambling on about what song to pick and what we're going to wear.

Chapter ● Thirteen

Juggling practice goes really well. A few hours in and I have a handful of new tricks under my belt, including a few partner passes with Riley. She spends the entirety of our time training together chatting about what we're going to do for the talent show. She's dead set on us performing some pop song I've only heard once. I say we should just do a song from *Wicked* and call it good.

"It's classic," I say. "Besides, 'Defying Gravity' would be pretty perfect, all things considered."

Riley rolls her eyes and tosses a club at my face. I catch it and toss a second to her.

"It's overdone," she retorts. "What about something a little less mainstream?"

"Mainstream? You wanted the pop song," I say, keeping up

the toss and catch. "Besides, I've sung this in front of an audience before. It won't be as bad as a song I barely know." My next toss goes long.

Riley fumbles the catch and races to grab the club as it rolls away. When she snags it, she jogs back across the tent, darting between a few kids tossing neon rings back and forth to one another.

"You need to work on your force," she says, giving the club a little flourish. "We may have our artistic disagreements, but I prefer not to get a nose job this summer."

"Sorry."

"It's fine. Practice makes permanent. And you'll practice until you're permanently awesome."

The four of us sit together at lunch, Tyler and Kevin and Riley and me. The moment Riley mentions doing a musical number, Tyler's eyes light up.

"I've always wanted to do a musical," he says. Kevin nudges him. "What?" Tyler asks.

"Sometimes you're too cliché for your own good," Kevin whispers very loudly.

"Quiet, you. I could still bench-press any dude here. I'm so awesome I'm allowed a cliché or two," Tyler retorts. As if to accentuate his mad skills, he tosses a chicken nugget in the air and catches it in his mouth.

Riley giggles and throws another chicken nugget at him before he finishes chewing the first. This one just bounces off his forehead and into his salad.

"Totally smooth," Kevin says. Then he turns to me. "Anyway, I'm in. I can't dance to save my life, but that will just make you look better, right?"

"Oh, I won't be dancing. I'll be singing."

"You sing?" Tyler asks. "I didn't know that."

"I am a girl of many talents," I say. Tyler grins, but before I can ask why he looks so happy, I find out. Someone sits down beside me.

Branden.

"Hey," he says. "Mind if I join you?"

"Not at all!" Riley responds. I want to ask where Megan is, but I keep my mouth shut and smile instead. He's in a lime-green T-shirt and khaki shorts. There's a light sheen of sweat on his face, but his shirt is dry. Was he practicing shirtless? Just the thought makes my heart flip. Thankfully, Riley keeps the attention off me. For a very brief moment. "We were just discussing how Jennifer's going to blow everyone away with her singing tonight."

"So I heard," Branden says. "Girl of many talents, right?"

"Except for handling heights," I mutter. Because I'm not going to let that be the elephant in the room—I know he's still thinking it.

To my surprise, the statement doesn't seem to make him uncomfortable; most people get uneasy when they're called out on things they're secretly thinking, but he just shrugs.

"First times are always terrifying," he says. "Some you can't overcome, and some you just have to leap over." He gives me a knowing look, and I'm suddenly not entirely certain we're just talking about flying trapeze. And now my face is definitely going red.

"Anyway," Tyler says, making me look over to him. I want to mouth *thank you* for getting everyone's attention. "Have you decided on a song for tonight?" He seems to reconsider his question, looking between Branden and me. "And are you in, Branden? We could always use an extra backup dancer. Or singer, depending."

"I'm no singer," Branden admits. "Or dancer, either."

"Oh, come on," Riley goads. "Every amazing singer needs equally amazing backup dancers."

Branden bites his lip and looks at me—or maybe it's the other way around, which seems like it would have an entirely different meaning. The blush I was just managing to get under control goes wild. Whatever act we do tonight, I'm going to have to wear a lot of foundation, otherwise I'm going to look like a tomato every time I remember that Branden's dancing around onstage with me. A part of me really hopes he'll say no. The rest of me—the part that wants to rub this in Megan's face and get the boy and still manage to be a star this spring break—has every finger and toe crossed that he'll say yes.

"Sure," he says. And it's like my heart does a little vault into my throat.

"Wait, really?" I blurt out, because I'm not entirely certain he said it or I just imagined he said it.

"Why not?" he asks with a shrug. "Sounds like fun, and it sure beats the beatboxing I was going to do."

"Wait, wait, wait," Riley interrupts. "You *beatbox*?"

"Nope. I'm horrible at it." Branden grins. "This is saving everyone a lot of pain and embarrassment."

"Yeah, well, you haven't heard my singing," I joke. Though I'm pretty certain my singing is better than his beatboxing. I can't help the self-deprecating humor. When I'm on a roll, I'm on a roll.

He smiles wider and puts a hand on my shoulder. "I look forward to it," he says. He turns to the rest of the group. His hand stays where it is. His touch is a bubbly mix of heat and electricity. It makes me want to lean in to him and wrap his other arm around me—something I've never felt from a boy before. In the back of my mind, though, I'm acutely aware that just hours ago, he was arm in arm with Megan. It reminds me of Josh and the cheerleader, and I suddenly want to shrink away. What if Branden really is just playing me like Josh did? "When are we going to practice?" he asks.

And then everyone starts comparing schedules, trying to find a free hour in a pretty packed day. The show is at eight thirty. And after a lot of negotiating, we find a time slot that works for everyone. The only problem is, it's only for an hour after dinner.

Branden squeezes my shoulder again when he stands to go to

practice. He seems excited, as do Tyler and Kevin and Riley. I can't help but feel we've got a lot of work to do. Otherwise this is going to be a disaster.

I have half an hour free between lunch and my next round of juggling practice. I consider going back and calling my parents, but I don't really know what I'd say. I don't want to tell them about not getting into flying trapeze, not yet. I don't want to disappoint them. And hey, maybe if I get really good at juggling before the final showcase, I'll be able to convince them I *chose* not to do flying trap. It's too nice out to stay indoors, anyway. And I have a feeling that free time is something I won't have much of for the next few days.

So, while Tyler and Kevin and Riley head to do some drop-in acro workshop, I leave the school and head across the lawn, past the tents and the mats in the sun where people are warming up or throwing a Frisbee. I try not to think about where I'm actually going; if I do, I might wimp out and stop myself.

I slow down a few hundred feet from the trapeze rig, leaning against a tree and watching the kids and coaches practice. I don't think any of them see me, not from here, but I brought a few juggling balls just in case—always practice, Riley told me. And practicing is a perfectly legitimate reason to be out here.

"That could have been you," I mutter to myself, tossing a few balls back and forth as I watch the kids swing and flip from the trapeze. When Branden climbs the shaky rope ladder and reaches

out for the trapeze, my heart leaps with him. He moves so gracefully, so effortlessly, and when he finally lets go of the bar and
flips in the air, he soars like a bird. A very attractive bird. I'm torn
between being impressed with the way Branden moves and being
upset that I'm not out there with him.

I should have tried harder. I shouldn't have given up.

Branden goes up again and does another flip from the bar—a
double somersault, this time—and lands effortless on the net,
bouncing high in the air on the rebound. Even though I've already
seen him do it, it still makes me a little nauseated. Face-planting
toward the ground just doesn't look like fun. He rolls over the
edge of the net and gracefully drops the few feet to the ground.
He glances over at me when he lands. If he notices me, he doesn't
say anything, just goes back to the group of trapeze kids and sits
down in the grass.

That could have been you, I think angrily again. *But you had to
chicken out. It doesn't matter that he's going to help you at the talent
show—you could have spent all this time with him if you'd just tried
harder.*

One of the ball tosses goes awry, and the striped ball flies away.
I curse and head over to it, not taking my eyes off the grass at my
feet so no one can see my face—not that anyone's looking at me.

Which is why, when I find the ball, I'm surprised to see it's
covered by a foot.

A foot in a pale-blue flip-flop.

"Looking for something?" comes her unmistakable drawl.

I look up and brush the hair from my eyes to stare straight at Megan. Her blond hair's in a ponytail, and she's wearing a pale-blue leotard and white shorts. She looks like something out of *The Nutcracker*. "Or maybe you were just looking *at* something?"

I grit my teeth and hold out my hand. Experience has shown that it's never smart to try and fight back with a witty remark. *Not that she'd understand wit if it slapped her in the face,* I think.

"Cat got your tongue?" she says, smiling like it's the funniest thing she's heard in ages.

"I think you're stepping on something of mine," I say.

"Oh, this?" She bends over—without bending her knees, of course, which just reminds me I can barely touch my toes—and picks up the ball.

I hold out my hand. "Can I have it back?"

She shrugs elegantly. "Maybe. But first you're going to tell me what you're doing all the way over here."

"Just give it back," I say. Ugh, it sounds like I'm whining.

She arches an eyebrow.

"Let me guess," she says. "You're out here because you wanted to watch *him*."

I don't look where she's looking, not until she laughs.

"I know you've got the hots for him," she says. "I mean, it's pretty obvious. And I know you think he likes you, but it's all pity. I heard him talking to his friends. Said he looks at you like you're his little sister. Like he needs to protect you. He *definitely* doesn't look at you like you could be his girlfriend."

"Just give me the ball," I grumble. I can practically hear my teeth grating. Getting kicked out of camp is the last thing I want, but I can't help but feel slapping this girl would be a justified reason.

"He and I go way back," she continues. "Met at a camp two years ago. It was love at first sight, but distance always got in the way."

"If that's the case, why aren't you two dating now?"

She just shrugs.

"Sometimes it takes boys a while to realize what they're missing."

"So he dumped you," I respond. I don't know where the sudden fire comes from, but I'm tired of being toyed with.

"You don't know who you're messing with."

"Neither do you. Now give me the ball."

To my surprise, she drops the ball into my hand. She visibly composes herself, drawing herself up a little bit straighter.

"Of course. I'll also give you some advice: Stop trying to impress him. You're only making yourself look desperate."

Then she tousles my hair—painfully—and stalks off. I can't help but feel what little hope I have diminish with every step she takes. Was she telling the truth? Does Branden really think of me as a sister? If so, I might as well just give up now.

Chapter ● Fourteen

A re you feeling okay?" Riley asks. "You seemed like you were on Planet Zombie all through practice."

I shrug. It's after our final juggling session for the day, and yeah, we made a lot of progress, but no, my heart wasn't in it. As we head back to the main building for dinner, I feel like a failure.

"I think I'd rather be on Planet Zombie," I mutter. "Or better yet, I know someone who should go in my place."

She sighs and wraps an arm around me. "Let me guess: Megan?"

I nod.

"You can't let her get to you!" she says. "She's just a bully. A contortionist bully at that, which everyone in the circus world knows is a hundred percent worse than your normal school bully."

"She said Branden thinks of me as a little sister." This just makes her hug me tighter.

"And how would *she* know?" she asks.

"She heard him say it. Also, apparently they dated."

Riley shakes her head. "I've seen the way he looks at you, and it is *not* like a sister, trust me. Megan's just jealous because Branden's spending all this time with you. Speaking of, we've got talent show practice right after dinner, so wipe that frown off your face before he sees it and thinks you're unhappy about performing with him."

I do my best to smile. It's one of those smiles that looks like a grimace, but it does make Riley laugh and murmur, "Hopeless" before opening the door for me. I'll take that as a slight victory.

"Okay, plan of attack," Tyler says the moment I'm sitting down. For a moment I can't tell if he *has* a plan or is asking for one, and it's not until after he's been silent for a few moments that I realize it's the latter.

"Can't a girl eat her dinner first?" I ask. It's lasagna tonight, and the smell of garlic bread has my stomach growling like an untamed lion.

"A girl *could*," Tyler says. "But then again, a girl could also get a big piece of pasta flung at her face if she leaves her boy hanging."

I snort and take a big, slow bite of lasagna, making sure not to break eye contact with Tyler while I chew.

"So ladylike," he says. Of course, that's also the moment when Kevin sits down next to him. Kevin's red hair is an even darker shade of orange—clearly, he just got out of the shower. The over-powering scent of body wash only confirms it. He nestles against Tyler's shoulder for a second before picking up his fork.

"Everyone excited for tonight?" he asks, as though he's oblivious to the interplay between Tyler and me.

"Totally," Riley says.

"Definitely," says Branden, who sits down beside me as he says it. I swallow my lasagna and nearly choke. He pats me on the back. "Careful. We can't have you choking before you're even onstage."

"Thanks," I manage. Once I get the coughing under control I look at him, looking at me. *Is* that how someone would look at a sister? I don't think it is, but then again, I don't have a sibling, so I guess I wouldn't know. And how the heck do I ask him if he actually dated Megan without it being awkward? "We were just deciding the plan of attack for practice."

"Well, first we need to settle on a song," Tyler says.

"We did," I begin, but he cuts me off.

"Too slow," Riley says. "Executive decision. You have backup dancers. So you'll need to sing something they can actually dance to."

I open my mouth to argue, but before I can get a word out, the guys are throwing different ideas back and forth. Not even a minute later they've settled on some pop song that's been taking over the radio all school year. The only input I get is when they ask if I know the song. Which I do. Luckily, it's in my range and luckily, I've sung it a few times. In my room. When no one was listening.

And just like that, it's been decided. We have a song.

That's when things go from bad to hilarious.

Because after the song's been decided, Tyler stands and pulls Kevin and Branden to their feet. At first I think it's to get more food, since they've already cleared their plates. It's not. It's to figure out choreography. It's been a crazy few days, and the moment Tyler starts swaying his hips and doing complicated arm gestures—much to the bewilderment of Kevin and Branden, who quickly stop trying to follow along—I burst into laughter. Riley snorts so hard she nearly coughs up her garlic bread.

"Stop, stop!" she chuckles. Tyler drops his arms with a scowl on his face. Branden and Kevin look at her like she's a saint. "Everyone's looking. We can't give away our secrets yet!"

"Fine, then," Tyler grunts. "I'm getting more food. I'll save the rest of my awesome for practice."

Tyler stalks off to the cafeteria line for more lasagna, and Kevin and Branden sit back down. Branden settles so close to me our arms are practically brushing. I glance over at him, to his spiked brown hair and gorgeous eyes, and in that moment I really wish our arms *were* brushing.

Of course, that's when Megan's treacherous voice floats through my mind: *He looks at you like you're his little sister.* I slouch away from him. Even when she's not there, Megan's good at ruining the moment.

Riley leaves a few jokes later, and Kevin's not far behind. Riley makes sure to pat me on the shoulder before stepping away, pointedly reminding me that practice is in thirty minutes and I should definitely not be late. At first I'm not entirely certain why she feels the need to tell me that—I'm kind of the lead singer, so it's my reputation on the line. Then Branden sighs heavily, and I realize it's just us at the table. Just the two of us. And Megan's nowhere to be seen.

"So," he says. There's an awkward tension in the air the moment I realize we're alone, like suddenly everyone in the cafeteria is watching us, listening in on every word we say.

"So," I respond, and poke at my lasagna.

"What were you and Megan talking about?"

Just hearing her name is enough to send a small jolt of fear and dread through me. I glance around; she's nowhere to be seen. It's almost like I'm worried that saying her name will magically summon her, like an evil genie or Bloody Mary.

"What do you mean?" I ask, looking back to him. He actually looks a little concerned. Wait, why is he looking concerned? Is there something she and I *shouldn't* be talking about?

"I saw you earlier, out at the practice field. You two were talking about something. Either that or you were just creepily watching us practice in silence."

I shrug.

"We don't really talk. I think she's set on us being mortal enemies."

"Ah, so threats then?"

I don't want to get into this, mainly because it would mean

admitting that I have feelings for him. And that Megan's trying to get in the way.

"It's nothing," I say. "I can handle it. She was just being herself. Anyway, how was the rest of practice?"

"You're avoiding the question, but it was good."

"Are you doing an act for the final show?" I push some lasagna around on my plate—not because I'm embarrassed to eat around him, but because the mention of Megan instantly made my appetite go away.

"Sort of. It's kind of hard to do an individual act on flying trap, so we're doing one big group number. Should be a lot of fun."

"I bet," I say. I can't help but let my voice get a little disappointed.

"How about you? Riley says you two are working on a killer partner routine."

"That's the goal," I say. *Not as impressive as flying with you, but I suppose it could be worse.*

He goes silent for a moment. I wonder if I should ask him about going to camp with Megan, but I honestly don't want to say her name aloud any more than I absolutely have to. I don't want him to confirm that they dated, or that they still kind of are dating, or that he's not sure of anything right now. Him being uncertain might actually be worse than him just playing me. I've read enough books about love triangles to realize that being the "other" interest always puts you in the friend zone.

"So what do you do when you're not here?" he asks.

"What do you mean?"

"Like, when you're just normal girl Jennifer and not circus star Jennifer. Do you play sports? Head the chess team? Solve local crime?"

I giggle in spite of myself, trying to pull my thoughts up from the deep. He's grinning at me. The smile's stupidly infectious.

"Something like that. Why?"

"I'm just trying to get to know you," he says. He nudges me. "After all, this camp isn't going to last forever. I'm trying to see if we'll still be in touch when it's done."

I glance over at him. Does that mean what I think it means?

"Well," I begin, looking back to my plate, "I'm in band. I'm not that good, but I just started, so I suppose that's okay. Mostly, I just do homework and game with my friends." I chuckle. "Totally cool, right?"

"Totally," he says. "I mean, what else are you supposed to be doing with your time? This is suburbia. It's not like you're gonna be driving around in a limo every day. Unless you have a limo. Then you should totally be driving around in it. Do you have a limo?"

I laugh.

"No limo, sorry."

"That's okay. You'd probably be a snob then, and I don't usually like snobs."

My treacherous heart does a little dance. Did he just say he likes me? *And if that's true, why the heck did you date Megan!?* Or was that just a lie? I wouldn't put it past her, but I hate how easily she's snaked into my brain. I want to trust Branden, really. But after what Josh did, it's hard. Much easier to keep it light and simple and pretend we're just friends.

"What about you?" I ask. "What do you do when you're not defying death?"

"Well, when you put it like that . . . I dunno, I'm an average guy. I'm on the swim team, play video games with friends, try to finish my homework last minute. Besides the trapeze stuff, I'm not very exciting."

"Sounds pretty cool to me."

"Pretty cool. Great, she thinks I'm *pretty* cool."

I nudge him and giggle.

"You know what I mean," I say.

"Hah, yeah. And you're pretty cool too."

I bite my lip. Suddenly he feels really close. Like, if this was a movie, this is where he'd push aside our dinner trays and lean over and kiss me. And suddenly that's all I can think about—him leaning over to kiss me. It's like everyone else in the cafeteria has disappeared and it's just him and me. So much for thinking of us just being friends; right now, I want us to be something *more*. Then something crashes and a bunch of kids laugh, and the moment is over before it even really began. He clears his throat and leans back—I hadn't even noticed he was leaning toward me; *was* he really about to kiss me?

"Anyway," he says, looking at his wrist—where he conveniently is missing a watch. "I better get going. Gotta call my parents before practice. And change. Apparently we're wearing short shorts. So that's exciting. Remind me never to let Tyler plan costumes again. He and Riley together are a powerhouse of embarrassingly bad ideas."

"Tell me about it," I say. "I'm just hoping it all pulls together by tonight."

Branden smiles. "I'm sure it will. If nothing else, your singing will blow them all away."

Then he stands and walks away, leaving me to sit there and wonder if that really was my first time honestly flirting with a boy.

Well, with a boy who flirted back.

Chapter ✿ Fifteen

don't stick around too long after Branden leaves. After heading back to my room to send my parents a quick update text, I leave and go straight to the practice area—just a small patch of grass behind the school where I'm pretty certain the college smokers go, given all the cigarette butts on the ground. I'm met there by Riley, who's doing her usual juggling by herself. This time she's not actually juggling, though apparently it's still considered "object manipulation." She's playing with a diabolo, which is basically a spinning top she wraps and tosses from a string held between two sticks.

"Hey, slacker!" she calls when she sees me. She flings the diabolo high in the air, spins twice, and catches it on the string right before it hits the ground. "Wanna try?"

"That looks way too complicated," I say. "Besides, I'm trying to keep my focus on not choking or losing my voice."

"Yeah, that would bite," she says. She sets the diabolo down, carefully folding the string around the sticks. "Can that even happen?"

"No clue. But I don't want to find out."

"What I *do* want to find out is how the boys look," she says with a grin. "I had a feeling they'd all have short shorts, what with them being athletes and all."

I shake my head. As much as I can't believe I'm about to say it, I can't actually get excited over the thought of Branden as a backup dancer; I'm too worried about making a fool of myself in front of the entire troupe. Again. I'm pretty certain it's impossible to lose your voice in less than an hour, but it would be just my luck.

Thankfully, I'm not given much time to worry; the boys all arrive at the same time, chatting with one another as they make their way across the lawn. They're each in lime-green T-shirts and bright-white shorts and sunglasses. I'm pleased to see that Branden's even wearing the brown vest from the costume challenge—must mean he owns it, which is cool. He has a good fashion sense.

"How the heck did you guys have all that?" I ask. "I mean, you match pretty perfectly."

Tyler shrugs. "Never question a circus boy's wardrobe. We gotta come prepared for anything."

"That and we talked to our RA about pulling from the costume shop," Branden says.

Tyler slugs him on the shoulder. "Stop giving away our trade secrets!"

"Break it up, ladies," Riley says with a laugh. "We've got work to do. Tyler, are you ready with the moves?"

Tyler nods, suddenly completely serious. Kevin smirks beside him—clearly, Tyler's the only one who's really getting into this. I wish I had half his enthusiasm. Or Riley's.

"Okay!" she says, a huge grin on her face. "Tyler, I'm leaving you in charge. I've got the music whenever you want it. And Jennifer?" she asks, turning to me.

"Yeah?"

"Try to keep up. This boy's choreo is killer."

Practice goes way too fast.

Not that that keeps me from feeling completely overwhelmed in the little time we have. I'm sweating after only a few minutes of trying to follow Tyler's complex dance moves, once more wishing I'd done *something* to prepare myself for all this. Why hadn't I taken dance classes like my mom insisted? Or gymnastics? Or even track?

It's quickly decided that I'll stay in front and do only a minimal amount of moving—and always at well-cued points in the music, so there's no chance of me messing up. Well, less of a chance of me messing up.

On the plus side, even though my moves are shaky, the boys more than make up for it. Tyler's a natural teacher, and both

Branden and Kevin are apt pupils. That said, they're all sweating by the time Tyler's done running them through the routine a half-dozen times. At least I'm not the only one who looks like I got rained on.

Riley is playing the director, since she wanted to focus solely on her juggling routine, which apparently consists of hula hooping while juggling fake knives. Seeing as she's flinging blades—dull or not—by her face, I don't pressure her into joining us. I'd rather not have to show her where the ER is in this town. It's kind of a trek.

"Great job, guys," she says. "This is going to be amazing! Tyler, you're half a count ahead during the last thirty seconds. And Branden, if you could maybe try to smile so it doesn't look like you're dying onstage, that would be awesome too."

"What about Kevin?" Tyler asks, sticking his tongue out at him.

"Kevin's perfect just the way he is," Riley says.

"Told you so," Kevin says.

Tyler rolls his eyes, but he's cut short by Kevin leaning over and giving him a kiss on the cheek.

"D'aww, you're too cute," Riley says.

Tyler responds by pulling Kevin into a dip and kissing him full on.

"Okay, okay!" Riley yells, giggling. "Get a room, you two."

It's adorable, but at that moment I look over to Branden. His eyes flick to catch mine, and something makes butterflies explode in my chest. Eventually, he looks away. I'm pretty certain his already flushed face goes a little redder.

This is exactly how I felt at the dinner table, only much stronger. And suddenly all I can think of is how perfect it would be if tonight, right after we were amazing onstage, he could sweep me into a kiss. He must feel it too. There's an electricity running between us, even though we're not making eye contact. A pull. Like magnets, I feel the desire to inch toward him. I mentally cross my fingers and hope that tonight's the night I get my first kiss. Spotlights and all.

Screw Josh and those mental games. Tonight's the night I get over him and move on to being with better guys.

"Earth to Jenn," Riley says, nudging me on the shoulder. "You still in there?"

I shake my head. Crap. I was staring right at Branden. Thankfully, he was too busy practicing a turn with Kevin and Tyler to notice. I hope.

"Yeah, sorry."

"Come on," she says, following my gaze. "Let's go get you changed. It's your big night, after all." Then she winks, and I have a funny feeling she knows exactly what I was daydreaming about.

That just makes me blush harder.

Chapter ● Sixteen

There's really nothing more nerve-racking than being in a talent show. Let me rephrase that: There's nothing more nerve-racking than being in a talent show and going *last*.

For some reason, Riley opted for us to take the final slot in the roster, which I think is a terrible idea but she seems to believe means we'll make a lasting impression.

"Come on," she coerces backstage, "this way you'll be the last thing everyone's thinking about."

I shrug. "It doesn't really matter, does it?" I whisper. "I mean, if this was just to impress Branden, we've won—he's already in the group!"

She shrugs her shoulders and tosses a knife in the air, catching it without even looking. Her solo act was a few routines ago; she pulled it off without dropping a single knife or hula hoop.

"Dream bigger, Jenn. This isn't just about impressing Branden. This is about impressing *everyone* here, including Megan. Once she sees you two onstage together, she'll get the hint. Then it will be nothing but loving looks and kissy-poo time with Branden for the rest of camp."

I actually snort with laughter. "Did you just say 'kissy-poo'?"

She grins. "You'll be coming back next year," she says, like there's no question at all, "and this will show everyone else who returns that you're multitalented. Coaches *love* that sort of thing. Who knows, they might even have you sing for next year's show."

The thought of that much pressure makes me want to throw up, so I focus instead on Branden, who's on the other side of the backstage wing. We're on in two acts, and he's peering at the group onstage—a clown troupe, naturally, doing some skit with a squirting umbrella—with almost as much nervousness on his face as me. Seeing him brings back all the butterflies from before, but this is a nausea I'm okay with. I can deal. Tyler and Kevin are nowhere to be seen.

We applaud when the clowns are done; they're all soaking wet, and their bows get the front row of the audience even wetter. I'm really grateful we're back here and not out there. Riley dressed me up in a sequined gold top that reaches my thigh, and tiny black shorts you can barely see past the hem. That, paired with some gold flats and a half-dozen bangles—not to mention all the makeup she splashed on me—and I feel like a rock star. Let's hope I actually look like one and not just like one of those clowns out there.

I refused to let myself look in the mirror beforehand.

Someone brushes past me and shoves me to the side. I stumble and look back. Of course. Megan and her sisters.

"Sorry," she says with a smile that says she isn't sorry at all. "I didn't see you there. I thought you were just a pile of discarded glitter."

"Leave off her, Megan," Sara says. I know it's Sara—it's the same sister who gave me that weird, almost-apologetic look earlier. Megan glares at her sister. Why in the world is Sara defending me?

"What are you doing back here?" I ask instead.

She just smiles and adjusts her top—a low-cut white thing that my mom would never have let me leave the house wearing.

"Performing," she says, then she and her sisters take the stage. Sara mouths *sorry* before stepping into the limelight.

I don't know what's worse: seeing Megan onstage, surrounded by her gorgeous blond sisters, and knowing that even Branden's eyes are stuck on her, or knowing the moment her music starts that she's stolen my song.

Riley starts cursing under her breath immediately. I don't think I've ever heard her swear, but she definitely knows a lot of colorful words. And I won't lie—they describe my feelings toward Megan pretty perfectly.

Tyler shows up right then, and he's just as flushed as I am.

"I can't believe this," he hisses, watching the girls from behind the curtain. "They stole the song!"

Sure enough, Megan's sisters are performing the same song and complimenting it with some scandalous dance moves. There are definitely more hip undulations than in our routine.

"At least she can't sing," Riley mutters, visibly trying to calm herself.

And yeah, that's true; I'm definitely a better singer than Megan. She's flat on almost every note, and when her sisters drop in for backup vocals, they're too sharp, which just makes everything sound horrible. I can tell that no one really cares, though. The audience isn't focused on the girls' singing; they're focused on their outfits and movements, which are almost worse than when they did their contortion act at the beginning of the camp.

"Can you believe it?" Tyler scoffs. "Does the girl have no shame?"

"I'd say that's a negative," Riley responds. "How in the world did they know what song we were doing?"

When I look to Branden, I realize he looks as deathly pale and upset as I feel.

I can't actually talk. I know if I do, I'll say something I shouldn't, or run out there and push Megan offstage. Thankfully, I don't have long to wait. Maybe it's rage or maybe they just did a shortened version of the song, but after what seems like forever and no time at all, they assemble for one final pose. The music cuts out and they bow as one, then saunter offstage. Megan makes sure to wink at me when she leaves.

"Knock 'em dead," she says. Then, before I can respond, Riley pushes me onstage and I'm blinded by the lights.

I don't have time to be angry. I don't have time to yell at Megan. But the moment the music starts and I pick up the mic, I *do* have just enough time to feel embarrassed. The stage lights make it hard to see the audience, but I can tell that they're shifting in their seats, wondering if there's been some sort of mix-up in sound cues. When the music keeps going and the boys take the stage behind me, I'm pretty certain someone out there snickers.

Then, before I can psych myself out and run offstage, my cue hits, and I open my mouth to sing.

Something takes over then, something I've felt only one other time—the last time I was onstage, singing for an audience. It's like all the fear and hesitation from before just melts away, and everything is easy and natural. Even though Megan and her sisters stole my song, the moment I get in the zone, none of that matters.

My voice is cooperating. I hit every note. I even manage to follow along to Tyler's intense choreography. At one point, I leap up into Branden's arms and he spins me around; being in his arms makes warmth flood through me. I spare him a quick glance; even though his eyes are on the crowd and sweat beads his forehead, he's smiling. For some reason, that image of him, shining under the lights, burns into my memory. When he sets me down beside Tyler, I know without a doubt that I'll remember that moment forever.

My adrenaline pumps and I want this to last forever—singing to the crowd, dazzling under the lights. But soon the music ends, and the boys and I take our bows and run offstage. The roar of applause follows at our heels.

"You were amazing!" Riley shouts the moment we clear the curtain. She runs forward and jumps into my arms—I just barely manage to catch her without toppling over. The boys are right behind me, and they all wrap their arms around us in a huge hug. From the corner of my eye, I see Megan scowling at us. Then she turns and stalks away.

"I didn't know you could sing like that!" Tyler yells, bouncing up and down.

"Neither did I!" I say.

For a few moments we just stand there, hugging and laughing. Then Riley pulls Kevin and Tyler away and tells them they need to go meet their adoring fans. Branden stays back with me.

I can still hear the scattering of applause from the audience, but it's quieter now that people are starting to leave and mingle. There will be snacks in the lobby, apparently, and then we have half an hour before sign-in.

Branden stares at me, then the ground, then back to me, and there's something in the way he's standing and fidgeting that tells me he's crazy nervous. My heart is still hammering away in my ears from post-performance adrenaline. But I know it's now mixing with another sort of excitement.

"You were, um, great," he says to the floor.

"Thanks," I say, because my New Year's resolution was to start accepting compliments. "You were too."

He grins and looks at me. The magnetism between us is even stronger. He takes a step forward, so there's only a few inches separating him and me. I know this moment; I've seen it a hundred times in movies, read about it in every book. This is the point where we kiss. This is the moment when the thrill of show business brings us together.

But then the grin slips, and I have this horrible feeling I've done something wrong. Do I smell bad? Is my makeup running?

"Jennifer, I . . ." He stutters to silence.

"What?"

"I have to be honest with you. I think . . . Megan knew what we were doing because of me."

It's like a slap to the face, one that magically strikes my heart as well.

I step back.

"What?"

He doesn't look at my eyes.

"She was talking to me after dinner. I mean, she cornered me, really. Asked what I was doing, tried to get me to join her for some partner acro stuff like we did at camp a few years back. I told her what I was doing instead. I didn't think anything of it, because I was just trying to show her I wasn't interested, but . . . Please don't be mad."

I take a deep breath I hadn't realized I was holding.

There's a part of me that's angry. Really, really angry—not just because he told her, but because he was talking to her, because they have some sort of connection that stretches far beyond this camp. So maybe it's not just anger, maybe it's jealousy. I want to yell at him, but I don't. Mainly because there's a look in his eyes that says he really is sorry. A look that makes me want to hug him and say it's okay, because clearly he sees my anger. He knows I want to throw a punch.

And that's the rest of my emotion. I want to comfort him. Because even though this sort of feels like when Josh stood me up, Branden's still here, standing in front of me, waiting for my verdict.

Sadly, I don't have time to give it.

"Oh, there you two are!" comes Leena's voice. "I was looking all over for you. You guys were fantastic!"

And just like that, the moment is shattered. Leena steps up between us and puts a hand on each of our shoulders.

"Now come on," she says. "Your fans and friends await."

She guides us out of the backstage area. I glance at Branden and catch his eye. He looks as embarrassed as I feel. And once Leena brings us into the lobby, I know whatever moment Branden and I just shared is gone for good. He vanishes into the crowd almost immediately. He doesn't even say good night.

When Riley finds me and brings me over to a group of campers huddled by the snacks, I can't focus on the cookies or conversation. I can only stand there and look around, trying to catch sight of Branden and wondering if I just royally screwed something up.

Chapter ● Seventeen

I don't see Branden for the rest of the night. Riley tries to keep me occupied with small talk and introductions to some other kids in the troupe. I do my best to smile and follow along, but I can't help but feel horribly disappointed in how the night turned out. Branden seemed genuinely sorry for talking to Megan. But if there's still something between those two, how can I trust him?

Riley's giddy when we're back in the room; she bounces back and forth and juggles random objects as she gets ready for bed. When she stops and actually looks at me, however, her energy drops a few notches.

"What's wrong?" she asks. She flops back on the bed, suddenly serious.

"I don't know," I respond. I turn away and start taking off the layers of makeup.

"Was he a bad kisser?" Riley giggles.

I shrug.

"Like, you're not sure or it was so bad you don't want to think about it?"

I set down the makeup wipes.

"Like, he didn't kiss me."

"Oh," she responds. Her tone goes flat. "What happened?"

I shake my head and go to the closet to change into pajamas. "Nothing happened," I say as I pull off the glittery top. "We were backstage, and I thought we were sharing a moment and then Leena appeared and ruined it. And *then* Branden just disappeared, like he was embarrassed to be seen in the same room as me. Oh, also, apparently he was talking to Megan and accidentally told her what we were doing. *That's* how she and her sisters found out."

I throw the dirty clothes in the hamper and turn to her.

"Am I crazy?" I ask. "I mean, I want to punch him and I want to kiss him and I hate that he and Megan are like old friends or something. This was supposed to be a fun week of flying trapeze. Why did it have to get all complicated all of a sudden?"

"If boys are involved, it's bound to be complicated." Riley pats the bed beside her. I flop down and lean against her shoulder. "And no," she continues. "You aren't crazy. It sounds like Branden's torn right now. But I really do think he likes you. It's not like he told

Megan our routine and then joined her side. He still followed you."

"So why does it hurt?"

"No one likes feeling like their trust was broken," she says. She wraps an arm around my shoulder. "Especially girls like us, who've had it broken before. Maybe he doesn't actually know what he wants," she says. "Boys are terrible at figuring out emotions. It's in their genes or something."

"What would you do, if you were me?" I ask. "I've tried to impress him, I've tried playing hard to get. And an hour ago we were dancing onstage together. I don't really know what else to do."

"You could always tell him you like him," she recommends. "I mean, maybe he's scared?"

"Scared? Of me? That's ridiculous."

"Boys fear rejection too, you know," she says. "At least, that's what Sandy says. According to him, boys and girls are actually pretty even in the emotional uncertainty department. Maybe that's why he still talks to Megan—she's his fallback."

"I can't believe your boyfriend actually admits to stuff like that."

"Oh, we talk about everything. Honesty's the best policy and all."

"So you're saying I should just come out and tell him I think he's cute and I daydream about him kissing me?"

This makes Riley laugh.

"No, that sounds creepy. We don't want to scare the poor boy off. I'm just saying that maybe you need to step up to the plate on this one. Tell him you like him."

"That's supposed to be his job," I say grumpily.

"Yeah, well, this is showbiz. Everything's topsy-turvy here."

In spite of the congratulations that still come my way at breakfast, I feel sluggish. Depressed. I even take a mug of coffee in hopes it will give me a bit of energy. I *never* drink coffee. It tastes like mud.

"Couldn't sleep?" Tyler asks. I pour another packet of sugar into my coffee, hoping it will help. Another sip. It doesn't. How do people *drink* this stuff?

"Yeah," I grumble.

"Must be all the adrenaline," he says. "Makes it hard to get any shut-eye."

He himself looks perfectly chipper—gym shorts, jersey shirt, and hair still damp from the shower. Kevin's in line for breakfast. They did an omelet bar today, which is pretty cool, save for the fact that I'm really not hungry.

"Anyway," Riley says, bursting through my sluggish thoughts. "Did you see what's on the schedule for tonight?"

"Not another talent show," I mutter.

She laughs. "Nope. Better. We're going to see a circus!"

I look at her, raising an eyebrow.

"There's another show in town?"

"Not really. It's, like, an hour away. But I've heard all about it. It's supposed to be really good. It's about a penguin trying to get back to the Antarctic."

"They made a show about that?" Tyler asks. "Also, Jennifer,

you're ruining your coffee." He reaches across the table, slides my mug over to himself, and takes a delicate sip. The face he pulls is comically disgusted. "Ugh. Way too much sugar. You've officially turned this into candy." He slides the mug back over to me. "Speaking of candy . . . how did things go with Branden after the show? I saw the way he was looking at you."

I shrug. Out of habit, I glance around the dining room, but I don't see him anywhere. I didn't really scare him off, did I?

"Nothing happened," I mutter. "He just left. Riley says I should man up and ask him out myself."

"You could," Tyler says. "I'm all for gender role reversal."

At that moment I feel someone stand beside me. I figure it's just Kevin, back from breakfast, but then Tyler's eyes narrow.

"What do you want?" he asks.

I look over then, to see Sara, one of Megan's sisters, standing beside me.

"I'm just here to tell you, and I quote, 'You should maybe find yourself another man.'" She looks at me dead on when she says it; her accent is just as thick as her sister's, albeit a bit more annoying.

"I don't know what you're talking about," I say.

She sighs.

"I don't want to drag this out. I really hate it when Megan makes me the messenger. But she says to tell you that she's done playing games. He's choosing her and there's nothing you can do about it."

"Branden's a big boy," Riley says, sticking up for me while I try to untangle my tongue and my wits. "He can choose for himself."

"And he did. Last night. At the trapeze rig. Where he and Megan were making out."

"You're lying," Riley says.

"Trust me, I like it about as much as you. Megan's vicious. I've seen what happens to the girls who get in her way. If I were you, I'd just let this one go. There are only a few days left. You don't want to deal with the fallout for the rest of your life." She sighs again. "It's so stupid." She gives me what looks like an apologetic smile. "I thought your act went really well, by the way. She never told me she stole the routine. You did better. But it's not a fight you can win."

Chapter ● Eighteen

She's lying," Riley tries to convince me for the hundredth time. "She has to be."

I shake my head. We're walking toward the practice tent and all I can think about is Josh standing me up at the restaurant. I should have known Branden was playing me like that guy. I should have known this wasn't going to be the spring of love or spotlights. I'll be lucky if I make it out of this camp without making a complete fool of myself. How many people know about Branden and Megan already? How many people has she told?

"She's not lying," I say. "It makes sense. It's why he never made a move. Megan said he thinks of me like a sister. Obviously, she was telling the truth. He fell for her. He told her about our routine. Clearly, he wasn't that impressed at the end, and he went for her instead. He just felt sorry for me."

I feel sick saying it, but there's a note of truth in the words, like a part of me knows reason when I hear it.

Riley sighs.

"Just try not to think about it," she says. "You've got an act to prep and a show to rock. Don't let one boy ruin your entire vacation."

I nod, but that's easier said than done. First the trapeze, then Branden . . . it's like nothing I actually wanted to happen during spring break went right. I should have just stayed home. At least then I wouldn't be going through so much heartache.

"Come on," she says, nudging me. "You still got me. I'll make sure you have a great camp. First stop: juggling practice till your fingers bleed!"

I try to smile and let her lead me inside the tent. I wish I could share her enthusiasm, wish I could just let it go as easily as she does. But all through practice, I can't focus on anything but my own thoughts. I can only go over last night and wonder where I went wrong.

Then, near the end of practice, it hits me: I didn't do anything wrong.

It's just that there was never any competition. Megan was always going to win Branden in the end—she was talented and smart and gorgeous. She'd already known him for years. She went for what she wanted.

Believing Branden might go for me had just been a lie I was telling myself. And that lie had finally died under the spotlight of truth.

• • •

It's hard to concentrate on anything besides my overwhelming desire to be anywhere but camp. Not even Riley and Tyler's antics can cheer me up. I spy Branden sitting next to Megan at lunch, and that just makes it worse. He looks over at me, once, and gives me a sad smile. I don't return it, just look back to Tyler and try to follow along with whatever joke he's telling. I don't even have it in me to pretend to laugh at the punch line. I just sit there and stare at the table and wonder if it would be a bad idea to call home and have my parents pick me up.

"You're really letting this get you down, aren't you?" Kevin asks.

I hadn't even noticed him sitting beside me, I was so out of it. He gives me a comforting smile.

"Yeah," I admit. Both Riley and Tyler are totally caught up in their joke. It's like they're in their own little world.

"Well," he says, "I wouldn't worry too much. You're a talented girl, and gorgeous. What you did onstage last night showed the mark of a true star. If Branden is too blinded by some silly girl, it's his loss, not yours. Any guy here would be lucky to call you his girlfriend."

His words warm a side of my heart that had previously been numb. Had I ever been complimented by a guy like this? Told that I was talented and pretty? I mean, sure, he's gay, but that doesn't take away the sincerity behind it.

"You mean it?" I ask. I feel a little pathetic voicing it, but I'm not above feeling a little pathetic right now.

"Of course I do," he says. "I thought that the moment I met you. You're going to be big, Jenn. You just have to start having some faith in yourself. I do. Heck, we all do."

And then, in spite of everything, I smile.

"Thanks, Kevin," I say.

"Of course," he says. Then he leans over and wraps me in a hug.

"What did I miss?" Riley asks, poking her head next to mine.

I giggle.

"Get in here," Kevin says, and pulls her into the hug as well.

"Lovefest! I want to join!" Tyler runs around the table and wraps his arms around us, squeezing tight.

I fall into a burst of giggles.

Even though I still feel a little crappy after lunch, and even though I *do* go call my parents, I don't ask them to pick me up. Instead I tell them that I'm having a great time and that I can't wait for them to see the show on Saturday. Which, once I say it, I realize is only two days away. Two days! I have to put an act together in two days! When I hang up the phone, Branden is almost entirely pushed from my mind. It's hard to worry about boys when you have a routine to practice. Even when said boy is as perfect and frustrating as Branden.

When I leave my room for the practice tent, my bad luck turns even worse. I run straight into Megan.

"You know," she says when I've taken a few steps past her,

"Branden's a really good kisser. It's a shame he wasn't interested in you. Well, shame for you. It's definitely not *his* loss."

I turn around, rage boiling out of nowhere. The last thing I need, however, is to get kicked out right now, so I try to keep the anger in check. With my luck, Leena's probably in her room, overhearing every word.

"Why are you like this?" I ask. "Are you really that sad of a human being?"

Clearly, that's not what Megan was expecting. She raises one perfect blond eyebrow and gives me a look like she's re-evaluating me.

"Is that really the best you got?" she asks finally.

"You think you're so cool," I say, "but I've watched you in the cafeteria. The only people who'll talk to you are your sisters. So if *winning* Branden or whatever you think you're doing makes you happy, do it. I just hope you're actually happy."

Then, before she can make a good comeback, I turn and storm off down the hall.

"Yeah, well, you're ugly!" she calls. I just shake my head and don't look back. She's not worth the trouble.

In spite of the anger that's still shaking through my veins, when I find Riley again I actually feel kind of good about myself. I've never really stood up for anyone before, let alone myself, and it feels nice. Empowering. Especially since I didn't sink to Megan's level; I never knew revenge on the high road could feel so good.

"You look . . . actually, I don't know how you look right now,"

Riley says. "You're a strange mix between smiling and vengeful. Like some evil cat overlord."

I grin and pick up the juggling balls on the side table.

"I just had an *interaction* with Megan," I say, tossing Riley a few balls. The other kids in the juggling tent have already starting practicing; the air is filled with music and the thud of juggling props.

"That explains the vengeful," Riley says, tossing the balls back. This back-and-forth passing has become our warm-up; it's hard to believe that last week, I couldn't even juggle two balls by myself. "But where's the happy coming from? Did you punch her?" Her eyes light up at that, which just makes me smile harder. The idea of little Riley getting into any sort of fight is kind of hilarious. Though I'm sure she'd pack a punch if she tried.

"No," I chuckle, "I didn't punch her. I just told her off and wished her well and left her in the hall."

"That's . . . really strange. You do realize you're really strange, right?" She tosses the balls a little faster, and I hustle to keep up with the new speed. It's not the same tempo as the music, which really throws me off. "You're supposed to be all mean and witty, not give peace talks."

I shrug, which is amazingly hard to do while juggling. It nearly makes me miss a pass.

"It just didn't seem worth it," I say. "I'm not about to fight her, especially when I only have to see her another two days. After the show, she's history."

"What about Branden?" Riley asks.

I drop the pass. The ball rolls away, but I don't go to catch it—we're juggling seven now, and if I run for the missed ball, I'll screw up the rest.

"What about him?" I ask.

"Well, you still like him, don't you?"

I open my mouth to say, *No, of course not, why would I like someone who played me like that?* but then I realize . . . I *do* still like him. For some strange reason, I haven't given up on him, not entirely.

"Ugh," I say instead. I can't tell if I'm disgusted at him or at myself.

"That's what I thought," she says. "You're not very good at hiding your emotions."

"I don't want to talk about it, okay? Not right now." I glance around. Although the other kids are all intent on their practice, the music isn't loud enough to drown out the conversation. I know it's no better than school—they're probably listening in, waiting to have something to gossip about later. "Anyway, what's the plan for the routine? We've only got two days."

"Well," she says, doing a quick spin in place and just making the next catch. "I was inspired by your singing last night."

"I'm not singing," I interrupt quickly.

"No, no," she continues, "I meant more your moves. I think we should choreograph something, make it more of a dance and less of a normal juggling routine. I mean, how often do you see two chicks juggling together?"

"I don't know," I say. "I'm guessing the question was rhetorical, so probably not very often."

"Practically *never*," she replies. "Normally it's just guys who do partner juggling. Girls are expected to be pretty gymnasts and wear sparkles."

"I thought you liked sparkles," I say.

"Sure, when I want to be wearing them. Otherwise, it's the patriarchy, man."

I laugh. "Okay, okay, so to fight patriarchy we're going to do a dance juggling routine."

"Yep!"

"I don't see how that helps any."

"It probably doesn't," she says with a shrug. "But that doesn't mean it hurts to try! If nothing else, it will keep your mind off things."

"Wait . . . this isn't just some grand scheme of yours to get Branden back for me, is it?"

She gives me her most innocent, winning smile.

"Me? Scheme? Jennifer, it's like you don't even know me."

"Oh, I do," I say with a laugh. "And that's precisely why I'm asking."

She just keeps smiling and changes up the juggling pattern. I don't ask her again, but I've got a funny feeling I already know the answer.

Chapter ● Nineteen

By the end of that afternoon's practice, we have the rough skeleton of an act. Which is good, since according to our instructors, we'll have only one more session to practice our act before everything gets put together for the first run-through tomorrow afternoon. So, a few more hours to fine-tune, and then we get to practice with the rest of the camp. Then it's showtime.

"I can't believe it's almost over," I tell Riley as we walk to the cafeteria.

"I know," she says. "Stupid spring break not being long enough. But don't worry, we'll all still be in touch. This is just the beginning!"

In spite of her enthusiasm, I still feel low. I was getting used to the circus life—up early for breakfast and training, practicing all day, and hanging out with friends every night. It's going to be really hard to go back to normal school after this.

As we're heading back in, one of the acro boys I've seen hanging out with Branden jogs past. His short brown hair kind of glimmers in the sunlight.

"Hey, you're Jenn, right?" he asks, turning around and keeping pace.

"Yeah," I answer.

"You were awesome last night." He gives me a grin. "You've got a great voice. Anyway, I'll see you around."

Once he's turned around and headed into the cafeteria, I turn to Riley and give her my *what was that all about?* look.

"Looks like someone's making new friends," she says, wiggling her eyebrows.

I laugh. She loops an arm around my shoulder. "Kinda nice living in the spotlight for once, isn't it?"

I nod. "Especially when it's not for something embarrassing."

"Just wait until the end of our act," she says, giving me a squeeze. "It's going to blow everyone out of the water."

"You're really optimistic."

"Nope, I'm a realist. I just know."

We're in line by that point; the cafeteria is already filled with the other troupers, all of them looking a little winded and tired. But there's an energy here, an excitement, and I'm not certain if it's because we're about to go see a professional circus or because we're all part of one. I glance over and see Branden sitting at a table with his other acro friends. He's facing away, so he doesn't see me, but I still look away immediately. Riley catches my gaze.

"Ignore him," she says. "He'll realize he made a big mistake soon enough. Maybe even in time for the dance tomorrow night."

"So much for being a realist," I say. She doesn't respond.

We grab our dinner and head over to where Tyler and Kevin are already sitting. They seem deep in discussion, but when I sit down, it's clear they're talking about routines.

"I just don't know if we're going to have enough time," Kevin says.

"Time for what?" Riley asks.

"He wants to do a duo act. Hand-to-hand." Kevin doesn't seem very excited about it.

"I just think it would be fun," Tyler says. "You've already admitted to basing acro before, and I can easily handstand off you. All you need to do is not move."

"Sounds fun. And dangerous," I say. "Are you going to do a full act?" Because if my little experience has shown me anything, it's that these routines take loads of time.

"No way," Tyler replies. "The acro group is doing a big finale sort of thing after our individual acts. I just thought it'd be kind of cool to do some hand-to-hand during it. No one else is."

"No one else could," Kevin says with a smile. "Fine, twist my arm. I'll do it."

Tyler hugs him. "I knew you would! There's a hand-to-hand

act tonight that I'm hoping we can steal some tricks from."

"Um, I don't think I'm comfortable doing tricks you haven't tried before."

"Well then, we'll just borrow some choreography or something. Speaking of," Tyler says, turning to Riley and me, "have you two decided what you're going to do yet?"

I don't even have time to open my mouth and respond; Riley immediately launches into her grand plans for our act, including the music and a few moves she credits to Tyler.

"It's going to be fabulous," she finishes. "We tried some of the choreo this afternoon, and it fits with the passes perfectly."

"Do we have a theme yet?" I ask, because I can't imagine them doing a full show without any sort of story line.

"It's going to be really loose," Kevin says. "I overheard some of the coaches talking. They'll announce the official theme tomorrow, but I guess it's just going to be something like Space Exploration."

"Oh man, I hope so." Riley's eyes practically glow. "We could do our routine in space go-go outfits, kinda like in *The Jetsons*."

I laugh. "I don't own a go-go outfit. And I only watched *The Jetsons*, like, once."

She shrugs. "I'm sure the costume department will have something."

At that moment, someone slams into my back, making me spill the glass of milk I was holding all over my tray.

"What the—," I begin, then cut off when I hear Megan's snicker. I'm also pretty certain I hear Sara mutter, "Really, Megan?"

I try to take a deep, calming breath, but Riley beats me to the punch. Almost literally.

"Watch it," she warns, jumping to her feet. Her hands are clenched into fists, and she's glaring at Megan with spite in her eyes.

"This doesn't involve you, nerd," Megan says coolly. Her sisters flank her like a pair of blond bodyguards, though neither of them look entirely comfortable with what Megan just did. Especially Sara, who's staring at her sister like she's the biggest jerk in the world.

Which, of course, she is.

Riley's knuckles go white. Even Tyler and Kevin are standing on the other side, watching the show warily. I reach out and grab Riley's arm to prevent a swing. I'm still sitting down; I'm not about to engage in this. Not with all the coaches around.

"She's not worth it," I intervene.

"Funny, that's what Branden told me last night." Megan's words slash at my heart. Sara puts a hand on her arm, though Megan's not gearing up for a fight. Physically, at least. She's working the emotional damage angle. "Guess that's why he chose me."

I grit my teeth. My own hands clench.

"Is there a problem here, ladies?" comes Leena's voice. She strides up behind the sisters and places a hand on Megan's shoulder.

"Of course not, ma'am," Megan says, putting on her sweetest voice. "Jennifer was just a little clumsy, that's all. Leaned back and accidentally bumped into me. That's all."

Then she flips her hair and walks away, her sisters trailing obediently behind. Another apologetic glance from Sara. Which is fine and all, but I really do wish she could put a leash on her sister or something.

For a moment, all of us stand there, staring at the retreating sisters. Leena looks bewildered.

"There's always one," she mutters to herself. Then she shakes her head like she just caught what she said, her cheeks flushing pink. "Is there something going on between you two that I should know about?" she asks, going all businesslike again.

I shrug. "Not really."

Riley opens her mouth like she's about to protest, but I yank her arm and force her back to sitting down. She says nothing.

"Okay," Leena says, disbelief clearly laced through her words. "If something happens, let me know. We don't want any bad blood in this show." She glances back to the triplets, sighs, and looks to me. "Anyway, great job last night. We're looking forward to what you guys pull off for Saturday. Enjoy the show tonight."

Then she leaves.

"Ugh," Riley grumbles once Leena's out of earshot. "I really want to deck that girl." She looks to Kevin. "If only you were doing hand-to-hand with her. You could drop her on her stupid face."

Kevin tries to hold in his laugh.

"Just leave it," I say, before they can start complaining. "She's not worth the waste of breath."

Thankfully, they don't push the subject, and we go back to

talking about the show. Well, *they* do. I just sit there and stew silently. A part of me really wants to ask Sara what's going on. But I have a funny feeling that, nice to me though she is, she's still on Megan's team.

Which is interesting, because I don't ever remember signing up to be part of this game.

Chapter ● Twenty

've seen the Karamazov Circus every year for as long as I can remember, but the show we go and see—which is almost an hour away by van—is a completely different sort of spectacle. The Karamazov show was always in a big top; even though there were sparkling outfits and grand music and bright lights, it had a sort of old-world charm, like it was all kind of antique. But this show, which is just called Nine Limbs, is entirely different.

For one thing, the show takes place in a theater. Riley and the boys and I grab a row of seats together near the front and pass our giant tub of complimentary popcorn back and forth between us. The stage is curtained with light-blue fabric that almost lets you see what's going on behind it; there are shadows moving back there, shadows that look like people warming up and setting up props.

"This is going to be amazing," Riley whispers into my ear. Then she pauses. "Uh-oh."

"What?" I ask. But I follow her gaze, and the question is answered. Megan and Branden are sitting down a few rows in front of us. I can just see their heads sticking out above their seats. "Great." *Now I get to watch them make out the whole show!*

"Ignore them," Kevin murmurs beside me.

Thankfully, I don't have long to watch. A few moments later the lights in the theater dim, and the show begins.

Like I said, I've seen the Karamazov Circus for years. What happens onstage with Nine Limbs takes my breath away.

Once the houselights go dark, the shadows behind the curtain start to move in unison. The music is driving but somber, all instrumental, and the shadows join and separate, making shapes that look like buses and skyscrapers and taxis. Then the backlights go bright and the curtain billows away.

Everything that happens onstage is a gorgeous mix of dance and circus and theater. The first act is a duo acro pairing that is honestly beyond words. They leap and twist in each other's arms, the ballerina-like girl contorting into impossible shapes with her partner. It's breathtaking, and the aerial silks routine that follows is just as spellbinding. It's almost impossible to tell where one act ends and the other begins—everything weaves together, drawn by the gorgeous music and a trio of clowns that are dressed like lawyers.

Even though it's beautiful, even though it's impossible to look away, I can still see Megan and Branden. I don't see them kiss, but she does lean her head on his shoulder once the show starts. For his part, he doesn't wrap an arm around her. It's a small victory. Very small.

Still, their presence taints the entire show. By the time intermission comes around—right after a really fast-paced juggling act done by five guys to jazz music—my stomach is in knots. Megan stands and stretches, arching her back more than is probably needed. Show-off. Branden stands a moment after. She takes his hand and guides him out into the lobby.

"Did you want to mingle?" Riley asks.

"No, thanks," I respond. "I think I'll just stay here."

"Suit yourself."

She and the boys leave. I stand and stretch but don't leave my spot. It's stupid and I can't believe I'm hiding in here, but I really don't want to see Megan and Branden together. It's bad enough knowing they're out there right now.

Ugh. I'm so pathetic.

"Jenn?"

I turn around. It's the boy from earlier, the one who complimented me after practice. I almost didn't recognize him without his practice clothes—he's in a button-down shirt with a bow tie. It looks like he's going to the opera, rather than a circus. He starts walking down the row toward me.

"Hi, um . . ." I trail off, because I don't think I ever got his name.

"Luke," he says. He extends his hand. "Sorry, guess I never introduced myself before."

"It's okay."

"Enjoying the show?"

I glance around. The place is still empty, but I'm not really looking for anyone. Staring at empty space is just a lot easier than making eye contact with Luke; his gaze is intense, and I don't know the last time a guy's looked at me like that besides Branden. Like they say: When it rains, it pours.

"Yeah," I respond, not meeting his eyes. That's when I catch a familiar silhouette in the door. Well, two silhouettes—Branden and Megan have perfect timing. I look back to Luke immediately.

"Cool," he says. His hands are stuffed in his pockets, and for a moment he bites his lip, which makes him look incredibly young. "Hey, um. You seem really cool and stuff. Would you maybe want to go to the dance with me?"

I open my mouth, slightly aghast. Definitely not where I thought this conversation was going: I'm used to being the girl who'd be asked if her best friend was taken or not. Why in the world was he asking me? Especially when I don't even know him. I think of Josh and being stood up, wonder if maybe this is the same thing. I'm about to say no out of habit—I mean, obviously this is some sort of mistake or mix-up—but then I see the way Megan's clinging to Branden. They're only a few rows away. Branden makes eye contact with me for just a second, then looks the other way, somewhat abashed. That's all the sign I needed. There's no way he'll be asking me, and I don't want to be going alone. Even Riley mentioned having her boyfriend Sandy driving out for the dance and final show.

So, once Branden's within earshot, I turn on Showbiz Jennifer and give Luke my most dazzling smile.

"Sure," I say, beaming. "I'd love to go to the dance with you."

I keep smiling and hope—really, desperately hope—that Branden sees it. I don't know why, really. It's not like I want revenge. I just want him to see that I'm not lost without him. Even if I did wish it was him standing in Luke's shoes right now. This is precisely what I wish I could have done to Josh after he stood me up—showed him my life wasn't over, and that he was missing out.

"Great," Luke says. The nervousness fades from him in an instant. "Well, um, looks like the show's about to start. I'll see you later."

Then he makes his way toward his seat, brushing into Megan and Branden as he goes. He looks back at me before sitting down. The smile he gives is oddly comforting. When the show begins, I find I'm not so bothered by Megan and Branden anymore. Life might actually be on the upswing.

Later that night, when we're back in the dorm and Riley's finally stopped going on about the show (she didn't talk about anything else the entire ride back), I manage to tell her about Luke. I was considering not saying anything, but after we turned the lights off and I snuggled under the covers, I realized I probably wouldn't get much sleep if I didn't spill.

"Wow," Riley says when I've filled her in. "That's . . . kind of unexpected."

"I know, right?" I prop my head on my hand and look over to her. She's already cuddled in, a pile of juggling equipment littering the ground beside her bed. "He's barely spoken to me at all and then—bam! Do you think it's a trap?"

She chuckles. "I don't see how it could be. I mean, it's not like he's going to dump pig's blood on you or anything. Maybe he was just too shy to talk to you earlier. Guys can be shy too."

"Really? He doesn't strike me as the shy type."

"Take Sandy," she says with a dreamy sigh. "He slipped anonymous love notes in my locker for almost a month before finally actually saying hello. When he did, he blushed brighter than my hair. It was adorable."

"I still can't help but think this is something Megan put together."

"I'm sure she has nothing to do with it. I've never seen those two talking to each other. Why can't you just believe that Luke actually likes you?"

"Years of practice," I mutter.

"Yeah, well, retrain yourself. You're awesome. Luke recognizes it. Go with it!"

I sigh and reach up to turn off the bedside lamp.

"If you say so," I say. "But if this is a disaster, I blame it on you."

"Whatever you say. At least we've got one hurdle out of the way."

I turn off the light. "What's that?"

"We know you can dance."

Chapter ❦ Twenty-One

I tell Kevin and Tyler all about Luke asking me to the dance over breakfast the next day. Not because I want to, but because Riley forces me into it. They're just as reassuring as she was, saying that my performance was definitely worthy enough to grab any boy's attention. The whole conversation lasts maybe five minutes—then it's right back to discussing the show last night and the different pieces of choreography they want to incorporate into their act. Even Riley gets in on it, discussing some new passes she wants to add into our routine.

"But we perform tomorrow," I say, my gut dropping. *And we practice in front of everyone else this afternoon!*

She just shrugs. "Fortune favors the brave. What's the worst that could happen?"

"I lose an eye, or a tooth, or get knocked unconscious, or fall on my—"

"That was rhetorical," she says, laughing. "You'll be fine. If we can't work it out by lunch, we don't have to put it in."

"Right," I say. "I'm not so sure I believe you."

"I wouldn't," Tyler says, leaning across the table. "I know that look: You're stuck with her crazy ideas whether you want to be or not."

Practice that morning is a nightmare. Riley wasn't kidding about trying new tricks, and she also wasn't kidding about only putting in the ones that we master. The trouble is, that means she's not letting things slide; no, she runs the passes over and over again. *Mastery* isn't really an option—it's a demand. Every practice before this was filled with idle conversation about where we grew up and what movies we were looking forward to. She doesn't talk at all during this, save for calling out drills and telling me what I'm doing wrong. Her tongue sticks out between her lips with determination, and after an hour and a half, I'm not the only one sweating.

Still, after the first hour, we've managed to nail down three new passes. Even the coach, Jim, comes over to tell us he's impressed with our progress. This doesn't mean Riley backs off in intensity, though; she immediately begins working the new passes into our old routine, blocking us through choreography and counting beats and calling moves. It's a miracle I'm able to keep up. I think, after

Tyler's training for the talent show, my body somehow managed to figure out how to remember choreography. Which is very impressive, seeing as my lack of muscle memory was a huge reason I never took dance.

The last hour of practice is for getting the entire juggling group in sync. We need to fit all of our individual acts together into a cohesive whole. Thankfully, there aren't too many of us, and after a few minutes of chatting, we have everything basically plotted out. Riley and I are scheduled to go on first, since we already have everything choreographed to music. I could cry in relief—after spending all that time waiting during the talent show, I don't think there's any way I could do it again. I can only hope my luck holds and the jugglers will be among the first to perform, like in the show we saw last night. *Don't let us be the finale!* The rest of the jugglers will filter in after us, and a few are going to just do some passes in the background of Riley and me. It should be simple. Fun. We've got upbeat music and crazy tie-dye costumes dredged up from the depths of the costuming department. Kevin had been pretty off in his guess of theme: We're doing Psychedelic Seventies.

My adrenaline is high when Riley and I leave the practice tent and head toward lunch. My stomach is also grumbling like it hasn't eaten in a month.

"We're going to kill it tomorrow," Riley says, beaming. She slaps me on the back. "Just make sure you don't mess up the 'chocolate bar,' and we'll be golden."

"I'll do my best," I respond, once more wondering who named these moves. *No pressure or anything.*

"Hey, Jennifer!" someone calls from behind. I pause, feeling my heart drop to my toes. I turn and try to give Luke a winning smile.

"Hey," I respond. *Smooth, smooth.*

"How was practice?" he asks, catching up and matching my pace. I glance to Riley, who gives me a hopeful smile and a thumbs-up before walking a few steps away.

"It was good," I respond. Suddenly I'm really wishing eloquence was my thing. I was never this tongue-tied talking to Branden. He was just so easy to be around. "How about you?"

"Great!" he says. "Everything really came together last minute. It's gonna be explosive. I can't wait for you to see it."

"Likewise," I say. We're nearly to the door, and my skin is practically crawling at how awkward it is trying to make conversation with him. I just hope that he doesn't try to talk at the dance tonight. It's not that he's creeping me out or anything—I can't really put my finger on it, but it just feels weird. And now that Megan's not around to one-up, I'm starting to doubt my choice of saying yes to him. "Um, what are you doing in the show?"

"Cyr wheel," he says. "It's that big metal hoop thing. I get to spin around and try not to throw up."

I laugh, because I know that's what I'm supposed to do, but in the back of my head I can only think of Branden's Cyr wheel performance at the demonstration at the beginning of camp. It seems like forever ago, but it was only a few days. Crazy.

"Awesome. I don't think I could do that. I get sick on the tea-cups at Disney."

"Me too," he chuckles. "I don't know why I do it to myself. Maybe because it looks so cool."

We step into the cafeteria, and I catch sight of Tyler and Kevin already sitting at the table, talking animatedly. Tyler catches sight of me and waves.

"Well," I say, trying to come up with a non-insulting reason to leave Luke in the lunch line. I can't think of anything. "Guess I'll see you at rehearsal?"

"Guess so," he says. He sounds a little disappointed, but I don't know if I can stand much more time chatting with him. When I leave his side and head over to the boys, I realize why.

Branden stands up at a table near the back and my heart does a double take. Even though Luke asked me to the dance, even though Branden's apparently completely entranced by Megan, seeing him still causes butterflies in my stomach.

You still like him, I think. *And because of that, going to the dance with Luke makes you feel like a traitor.*

I shake my head and try to push the thoughts out of my mind when I sit down across from Tyler, but it doesn't help.

I still have feelings for Branden. And unless one of us makes a move soon, camp will be over before it comes to anything.

Chapter ✺ Twenty-Two

We start the group rehearsal almost immediately after lunch. As one, the entire camp assembles in the one tent none of us has stepped foot in since the camp started: the big top. Chills roll over my skin the moment we step inside; this is it. This is my dream coming to life. Today, even though it's still technically just a rehearsal, I make my debut as a big top performer.

I settle in on the bleachers beside Riley and Tyler. Olga is in the center ring, chatting with a few of the coaches. The rest of the staff is sitting on the ring curb—the red ring that encircles the carpet-covered stage. Once the entire camp is assembled, Olga claps her hands for silence. The whole tent goes still.

"This is it, troupers," she says, walking back and forth like a ringmaster taking control of the stage. "Today is the day all your efforts culminate into a show. You've all worked very hard for the last few days, but I'm afraid the hard work isn't over just yet. This is where your dreams become a reality. To get there, however, we'll need to push just a little bit more. I'm hoping the show last night inspired you to dream bigger, strive harder. You'll need that motivation for the training ahead.

"Over the last few days, you've not only learned new skills and routines, but you've also learned about your fellow campers. You've made new friends and creative allies, and hopefully you've discovered more about yourselves and your art form in the process. Our sincerest hope as your coaches and confidants is that this is just the beginning of your circus career. Consider tomorrow's show a stepping-stone. The applause is all yours, but it is just a taste of what's to come."

Then she begins to discuss the show order. My dreams of going on first and getting it all over with are short-lived. Juggling is right after the intermission, which means I not only have to wait through an entire first set, but twenty minutes of milling around with family and friends as well. The only perk is that my nerves will get a small puncture right away; the entire company will go on at the start of the show for an opener called the *charivari*. Apparently, this means I'll come out juggling and end in some group pyramid we'll be practicing soon. I just hope this means my stage fright will be able to take a backseat for the rest of the show—maybe the adrenaline will last?

And then, after a few minutes of discussing how the overall show will run, we get right into practice.

If I thought rehearsal with Riley this morning was work, group rehearsal is an entirely new level of stress. We spend a good thirty minutes blocking out the *charivari*, making sure everyone knows their entrance cues and choreography. Riley and Tyler and I do a three-person pyramid for our final pose that consists of me standing on both of their knees while they hold on to each other's hands in a sort of chair pose. I don't know the name of the pose, but I do know I wasn't made to do partner acro: It takes all my willpower not to shake so hard that I topple over. Turns out standing still on two people's knees is actually a lot of work.

The perk of this is that my focus is entirely on the work at hand. It's only when we take our first break that my brain switches over to worrying about later tonight. There's a small part of me that's still hoping Branden will dump Megan and ask me to the dance—not that I want to let Luke down like that—but when I look over and see him standing at the water cooler, those hopes drown. He's standing there with Megan at his side, her arm looped through his. As if on cue, he looks back to me right then and catches my eye. Once more, I can't figure out his expression; it almost looks a little apologetic and a little hurt. Then again, I'm probably just projecting.

Megan turns her head when he looks away and stares straight at me. She winks. I'm *definitely* not projecting there—her expression is smug, and it puts me on edge.

I turn away and spot Luke in the crowd, practicing back-flips with some other acro kids. He notices my glance and gives me a wave, then goes back to spotting his friends.

You're being ridiculous, I chastise myself. *A week ago you would have killed to have a cute boy ask you to a dance. And now you're dragging your feet because he's not the one you thought you wanted. Just give him a chance. You never know—he might be a real gentleman.*

So I swallow what little pride I have and convince myself to give tonight a chance. Stop hurting myself because Branden isn't stepping up to the plate and actually enjoy my time with the boy who did. It still feels like walking into some weird trap, but that's probably just nerves as well.

I know one thing for certain: Showbiz certainly messes with your perception of things. It's hard to tell where the stage ends and real life begins.

After the break, we go into the actual run-through of the show. It's our first chance to see everyone perform their acts, and the pressure is on. I mean, I know everyone's supportive—this is our collective show, and we all want it to be good—but I can still feel the adrenaline pumping through the tent. I'm not the only one who's never performed in a big top. I'm not the only one whose dream is about to be realized. Or trashed.

We run through the *charivari* once more and then disperse into the bleachers to block the rest of the acts. The clowns go on first, wearing some crazy tie-dye lab coats and saying they've discovered a way to go back in time. Their skit is actually really funny, and that's coming from a girl who usually doesn't like clowns. They don't do any pie-in-the-face humor. It actually has some wit to it.

Near the end, the three clowns stumble into their time machine—which is just a giant cardboard box decorated with stars and painted-on clocks—and the lights dim. The music changes to some time-warp-sounding synth. When the lights come back on, the clowns fall out of the box just in time to nearly get run over by the Cyr wheel group.

Luke and the other three performers—two girls and one other guy—are amazing. Luke seems to be the leader. As they all roll and spin around one another in perfect time to the music, he rolls to the center of the ring and starts spinning incredibly fast, cartwheeling at dizzying speeds before rolling around like a spun penny, going faster and faster and lower to the ground until I'm sure he's going to fall. He doesn't. He manages to spin back up to standing and then rolls back into the group for a few more tricks and spins. When they all stop and take a bow, I know I'm clapping louder than anyone else.

Suddenly the fact that Luke asked me to the dance seems like some sort of honor, like it's a miracle he even noticed me, let alone asked me out. I'm not normally one to look at the people around me like we're all ranked, but when I watched Luke perform, he definitely seemed like he was on an entirely different level. Out of my league.

If only I could convince myself that my singing actually was good enough to capture his attention.

Right after their act, the contortionists take the stage. My excitement from before immediately melts into a sick sort of envy.

The Triplets are stunning. They're wearing sleek checkerboard-sequined leotards and perform on a raised golden pedestal. When the music starts, they begin twisting all over one another, contorting into moves I'm pretty certain aren't humanly possible. I hear Tyler mutter, "Cyborgs," beside me, and I stifle a laugh. But it's hard to make fun of them; their act is solid. I sit through the entire thing with my mouth agape and this growing knot in my chest.

This is why Branden chose her, I think, as Megan does a one-armed handstand on top of her sister's raised leg. *She's talented. She's more than talented. She's a goddess. She takes risks. And you were too scared to climb a stupid ladder. What made you think you had a chance?*

If there's one thing I've learned, it's that I'm my worst enemy. I can't focus on the rest of the contortion act once those vile thoughts seep into my mind. Thankfully, the act is up before I can get too aggravated—both at Megan's smug grin and my own frustrating lack of courage. The next group to go on is the clowns again, but their skit is dulled by the dialogue racing back and forth in my head.

I should have just climbed that dumb ladder. Then Branden would have chosen me and I wouldn't be sitting here, wishing I was good enough.

But then some small, rational voice in me whispers that I shouldn't have to try so hard, that I should just be myself. After a few rounds of this back-and-forth, I realize it's not just about

Branden. This is about me. This is about being good enough for myself.

Not climbing that ladder meant I copped out on the one dream I'd been harboring for years. Branden was just a side note. The real disappointment was that I'd given up on myself.

And I wouldn't have another chance to make it right.

Riley taps me on the arm, snapping me from my reverie. I glance at her to ask what she wants, then catch the movement on the stage.

Branden.

It's time for the flying trapeze routine. Time to see just what, precisely, I was missing out on by being a coward.

Chapter ● Twenty-Three

Watching Branden do his routine is just another reminder of how far out of my league he is. After the coaches confer for a few minutes about the choreography and the flying trapeze net is rigged in place, he and the other performers begin climbing the rope ladders on each side of the ring. Branden goes up and mounts a trapeze first, flipping himself upside down and latching his legs to the bar. Just watching him makes my heart soar up into my throat. Vertigo snakes its way through my chest. My palms go cold and break into a sweat.

Branden swings back and forth a few times while another guy climbs up and grabs the trapeze on the other side of the ring. Branden claps his hands and the other guy jumps out on the trapeze, swinging fast toward Branden, until he reaches his peak and lets go, doing a double flip in the air and catching Branden's hands. My terrified heart stops during the entirety of that leap, right until the two boys' hands clasp and it's clear no one's going to fall to their deaths.

"He's good, isn't he?" Megan whispers from behind. I can practically hear the smile in her words. "So talented. So *brave*. I'm so lucky he asked me to the dance. I can't wait."

If my jaw clamped any tighter, my teeth would grind to dust. Branden switches off with another performer, completely oblivious to the two girls quietly warring it out over him less than fifty feet away.

At that moment, Riley steps in—she turns around in her seat and gives Megan a death glare.

"If you don't shut up," Riley whispers, "I'm going to use your eyes as juggling balls. Got it?"

Megan just laughs to herself and leans back in the bleachers. She smiles and waves, and my attention goes back to the center ring. Branden is staring right at us. He looks concerned.

Probably because Riley's face is almost as red as her hair. I think she's angrier than I am.

I shake my head and take a deep breath, try to force down the fight-or-flight response that—for the first time ever—seems to be geared toward *fight*. I don't know how Megan manages to get under my skin so easily, but I'm more than ready to have her out of my life. I try to focus on the trapeze artists. Well, all of them except for Branden, who's once more grabbing the trapeze and swinging across the ring. My palms are still freezing with vertigo. What made me think I could ever do that?

Maybe that's why Branden didn't ask you out. If only I could get Megan's taunts out of my head. I think I'd have a greater chance of getting her to apologize—like I said, I am my own worst enemy. And that's including Megan on the list.

The trapeze act finishes with every performer taking turns on the trapeze bars and doing insane flips, then plummeting to the net below. My pulse speeds up every single time they dismount. By the end, I'm actually a little glad it's over; I don't think I could handle much more adrenaline.

I don't know what brought on the switch. I always loved watching the flying trapeze before this, always daydreamed of doing all the daring tricks and flips. Maybe it's because I now know just how terrifying it is up there. Well, sort of. Halfway up the ladder doesn't really count.

The trapeze group filters off to the bleachers. Branden gives one more glance my way—or maybe it's at Megan, hard to tell and I don't really want to know—before sitting down beside Luke. Uh-oh. I know it's conceited to think they're talking about me, but when they both glance over, I can't help but think the worst. At least neither of them starts laughing and pointing.

Not that I know why they'd do that, but if this were a movie, it would be a prime moment for some embarrassing gesture, when Branden convinces Luke he picked the wrong girl.

"Nice work, everyone," says Olga. She steps center ring,

commanding everyone's attention. "That went incredibly smoothly, especially for a first run. Now we're going to take a ten-minute break to reset the ring for the second act. We have some snacks just outside the tent if you'd like to go stretch your legs. See you in a few."

Then she walks over to some of the coaches.

"Come on," Riley says as she stands. She grabs my arm and pulls me up, nearly dragging me out of the bleachers.

"You're going to rip my arm off," I mutter. But I don't drag my feet. *I* don't want to be sitting in those bleachers in front of Megan either.

Once we get outside, Riley heads straight to the snack table, which is covered in fresh fruit and granola bars and juice. She grabs an apple and stalks away from the crowd. I grab a granola bar and follow.

"I can't stand her," she says. She doesn't take a bite of the apple; she just tosses it back and forth between her hands. I'd never seen angry juggling before. Now I have. "I hope she falls on her stupid pretty face tomorrow."

"Jeez," I mutter. I snatch the apple from her, mid-toss, and bite it. "I thought I was supposed to be the angry one. I mean, she did steal my guy."

"I know. That's part of it. But she's just so . . . ugh!" She actually stomps her foot, her hands balled into fists. "She's so condescending and entitled and I hate her."

"Calm down, angry little pixie girl," I say. I hand her the apple, making sure the bite mark is facing her. She snorts with laughter when she takes it back.

"Thanks," she mutters. "Sorry. I should be comforting you. Do you need comforting?"

"I'm okay," I say. It's easier than admitting that I feel like crap.

"Liar."

I roll my eyes and look toward the tent.

"I don't know," I say after a pause. It's clear she's not letting me off the hook. "I just feel lame, you know? Like, I should have been up there with him. Them. I meant them. I should have been performing with the rest of the trapeze group, and instead, here I am, waiting on the ground."

"With me," Riley states. She sounds a little angry, and not from Megan. I look to her.

"Yeah," I say. "And I'm grateful for it."

"Listen, I know you're angry you aren't doing flying trapeze with Branden. I know you feel like a failure. But you're still doing something really cool with someone who thinks *you're* really cool, and she would appreciate it if you stopped treating the act like it was a chore."

I bite my lip. "Sorry. I do enjoy it. It's just not what I expected when I came here."

"That's life," she says. "You just gotta roll with it. If you're meant to do flying trapeze, you will. There's always a second chance."

"I hope so."

"In the meantime," she says, looping an arm around my

shoulder, "stop acting like doing a routine with me is so horrible. You're starting to make me feel bad about teaching you in the first place."

"Sorry."

"Stop apologizing. This is showbiz, and you know the first rule of showbiz."

"Er . . ."

"Keep smiling," she says, and drags me back toward the tent.

My hands are shaking as we wait backstage with the rest of the juggling group. Even Riley looks a little nervous—her usual grin is gone, and there's a furrow to her brow. I wonder if she's mentally going through our duo act or her solo routine for the grand finale—I wonder if part of her concentration is trying to figure out ways to cover my potential screwups. The area back here is tiny— just a small hall between the curtain and the back tent flap—and the heavy air is thick with anticipation.

Finally the music starts, and we burst through the curtain and into the ring.

Much like during the talent show, the moment I'm onstage, all the fear vanishes. The routine comes naturally—we dance into the middle of the ring, and Riley and I begin our complicated duo routine. Even though we've only practiced this a few times, the moves come out of habit, like I've somehow become a well-oiled circus machine. We toss and spin and catch, all perfectly in time to the upbeat music, while the rest of the jugglers do their own acts around us. I can practically feel the energy in the room amp up as the routine goes on.

When Riley and I do our final move and pose, the tent erupts into applause. We all stand there, sweating and breathing hard, soaking up the praise.

"Very nice!" Olga shouts, stepping into the ring. "That was a perfect performance. I don't think I have any notes, do you?" She turns to our juggling coaches, who both shake their heads, huge grins on their faces. "Well then," Olga continues, "let's move on to the next act."

We jugglers bow, then run back through the curtain.

"That was amazing!" I yell the moment we're outside the tent. The air is cool and the sun is bright—everything feels alive. Suddenly my depression from before and envy over Branden and the contortionists is gone. It's hard to feel down when pumped with this much adrenaline.

Riley runs over and wraps me in a hug. "*You* were amazing," she says. "I told you that you were made for the stage."

I step back and keep my hands on her shoulders.

"Thanks," I say. "Thanks for believing in me."

"Always," she replies. Her smile is huge. "Now I just need to get you to really believe in yourself."

I nod my head. "Working on it." And we head back into the tent to watch the rest of the acts.

Chapter ☙ Twenty-Four

I t's almost impossible to pay attention to the rest of the acts. The performance high is so powerful, I don't even feel the slightest hint of anger when Megan glares at me from her seat. Branden is still sitting next to his acro group, but I do notice him glance over to me now and again. My heart flips every time, but I let it go. I'm not going to let my interest in him ruin this moment.

After the individual groups run their routines and figure out entrance and exit transitions, the entire troupe goes back onstage to block out the finale. It's supposed to be high energy, so we are all coming out doing partner and solo bits before finishing with one large human pyramid. I'm doing some solo juggling right beside Tyler and Kevin, who are doing an abbreviated hand-to-hand routine. Performing beside them makes me feel even more talented—they're both so good, so strong and graceful, that I feel it rub off on me just by being near. Even sharing the stage with the Twisted Triplets makes me feel a small note of pride; this finale is about sharing the playing field, everyone on the same level. It means we're all just as good as the other performers.

I glance at Branden during the final pose. Of course, being onstage with him means trying to convince myself that we're on the same level as well, that he's not out of my league. *You're going to the dance with Luke,* I remind myself, and bring my focus back to the choreography.

When practice is over, I feel both exhausted and energized. I don't think I've ever worked so much in my life, but I also don't think I've ever felt so fulfilled by the process.

Riley and Tyler and Kevin head back toward the cafeteria immediately after. My stomach rumbles, but I need to put away some juggling equipment before heading in for the night. After all, the dance is later—there won't be any more practice for the rest of the day. I head toward the juggling tent and store the props in one of the multiple steamer trunks.

"Hey," comes a voice behind me. My heart stops with the slam of a trunk lid. It's Branden.

"Hey," I say. I stand and turn, slowly. I don't really want to be in the same tent as him, mainly because I feel like there's way too much left unsaid between us. And I don't really want to start now.

"I really liked your act," he says. His hands are shoved in the pockets of his gym shorts, and he refuses to meet my gaze. For some reason, this makes me stand up straighter. I don't want to feel like I'm the needy one, not anymore, and I'm trying to convince myself that if I stand tall, I'll feel tall.

"Thanks," I reply. I don't move toward the exit, even though I really wish I could. The warm air in here feels a little too close, a little too suffocating. "You were really good too."

"So I hear you're going to the dance with Luke," he says. It's so off topic it's like a blow to the gut. My mind reels as I try to form a fitting response.

"Yeah, well, he asked me," I say, trying to instill the words with meaning: *You were too busy making out with Megan. I was tired of waiting for you to man up.*

"Yeah," he says. "I heard that part."

For some reason, he sounds really hurt by it. A small piece of me wants to feel victorious. But mostly, I just feel guilty.

"I don't know what you sound so sorry about," I say. I don't know where the words come from; maybe I'm just tired of being kicked around. "You're going with Megan."

He shrugs and mutters something under his breath.

"What?" I ask.

"Nothing," he says. Then he sighs deeply and looks at me for the first time this entire interaction. "Anyway, I just . . . I just wanted to say you looked good today. You should be proud."

"I am," I say. "Thanks."

"I don't know why you're mad at me," he says. And yeah, I

suppose my responses were biting, but I'd hoped I was hiding it better than that.

I open my mouth to explain precisely why I'm upset, but then the tent flap opens and the reason for all my anger steps in.

"Oh, there you are, Branden," Megan says, stepping inside. My blood boils at the sight of her. She glances at me just once, giving me a look that says I'm clearly not worth any more attention than that, and focuses on Branden. By "focuses," I mean "walks up to and grabs his arm like I'm not even in the tent." She continues, "I was hoping I'd be able to find you before dinner. I wanted to make sure we matched at the dance tonight."

It takes all my self-control to keep myself from screaming at them as she flaunts the fact that *he* chose *her*. I try to hold on to that bubble of happiness from before, the exhilaration of a show well done. It's impossible, like trying to hold on to a greased juggling pin.

I don't need to stand here and take this. But I'm also not about to give Olga or anyone else a reason to throw me out because I decked a contortionist in the face. Without saying another word, I stalk from the tent, making sure to brush into Megan just enough to shove her to the side as I leave.

I'm sitting with Riley and the boys at dinner, trying not to think about Megan and Branden and having to watch them dance tonight, when Luke steps up behind me and places a hand on my shoulder. The other arm reaches around in front of me to hold out a flower. A little pink carnation. When did he have time to get me a flower? In spite of everything else warring in my head, that gesture of kindness makes me melt a little.

"What's this for?" I ask, looking up to him. He smiles down at me, completely oblivious to the rest of the table.

"Your performance today," he says. "I would have gotten a corsage for tonight, but turns out they're hard to find at a gas station, so this is the best I could do. That, and I didn't know what color dress you were going to wear."

I take the flower gently and feel my stomach drop. Does he *really* like me that much? If so, I feel bad for having feelings for Branden. Once more, I try to convince myself to give this boy a chance. He's certainly trying harder than any other boy in my life.

"I didn't bring a dress," I respond. I give him an awkward smile. "Sorry."

"Oh. Well then, a really good thing I didn't get you a corsage."

"She has a dress," Riley pipes up. "She's borrowing one of mine."

Luke's smile widens. "Excellent. I mean, not that it matters. I'm sure you'd look great no matter what."

Then, because once more it's nearly impossible to hold a conversation with him, he excuses himself and walks back over to his table of acro boys. Which, I'm pleased to see, Branden is sitting at. Without Megan.

"Jeez, girl," Tyler says, "how much clothing did you *bring*?"

Riley smiles and pops a carrot stick into her mouth and

responds around her crunching. "A girl must always be prepared."
Then she glances at me. "Clearly, this is yet another skill I must
verse you in. At least now I *know* I'll see you outside camp."

"Really? Why's that?"

"Because you still need a lot of work before you can call yourself a lady."

I just giggle and shake my head; it's hard to take her seriously
when she still has half a carrot crunching in her mouth. If I'm taking lessons from her, it will be years before I can consider myself
proper.

There's not much time to prepare for the dance after dinner, so
Riley and I finish eating early and head to the dorm immediately.
She forces me to take a shower before she does, convinced that
it will take me extra time to make myself presentable. Which is
probably the truth, seeing as she's going to be the one dressing me.
And doing my hair. And my makeup.

If I make it to the dance without looking like a clown or having purple streaks in my hair, it will be a small miracle.

She's already laid a few dress options on my bed by the time
I've stepped out of the shower. I reiterate Tyler's earlier question
when I see the three choices: "How much clothing did you *bring?*"

"Barely enough," she says, sounding sad. She hops off the bed
with her towel in hand. "Try them on while I'm in the shower. I
expect you to be ready for hair and makeup by the time I'm out.
Unless you choose poorly. Then it's back to the drawing board."

She pats me on the shoulder and bounces into the bathroom.

The dresses she picked out are definitely Riley. There's just enough of a clash in colors and patterns to edge on gaudy, but she has a keen enough fashion sense that they actually, miraculously, work.

Option one is a slinky lime-green sundress, paired with a leopard-print belt and a sheer yellow shawl. She even set a pair of giant plastic bauble earrings beside it—they look like pink grapes.

Option two is a long pink-and-purple plaid skirt with a white blouse and a purple jacket that looks like a short ringmaster coat. She's paired it with a studded pink belt and a necklace made of thick silver squares.

Finally there's a relatively plain cream-colored sundress with a delicate blue embroidered hem. It would have been the sanest of the options, but she's paired it with a rainbow-tie-dye shawl and multicolored plastic bangles. It's the only option that has shoes to go with it. Apparently, if I'm to wear this, I have to also wear her pink, marker-covered, knee-high sneakers.

I decide to try on the green sundress first. I'm lucky Riley is my size—the dress just barely fits, but it doesn't really mesh well with my skin tone. As I stare at the ensemble in the mirror, I can't help but wonder how in the world she manages to pull this off without looking like a Christmas advertisement. The green with her red hair would be a color clash waiting to explode.

The cream dress is next, mainly because I think my eyes need a rest from all that intense color, and the plaid dress just screams disaster to my relatively conservative fashion sense. But looking in the mirror, fully decked out, I can't help but think it's almost a little *too* plain. I thought I would have settled on this one, but it doesn't scream "Jennifer, Juggling Circus Star." It just whispers "Jennifer, Still Too Scared to Take Chances."

So, almost a little regretfully, I slink out of the cream dress and try on the pattern explosion of option two.

Of course, that's the moment Riley gets out of the shower, a towel wrapped around her and another around her wild hair.

"That one," she says, casting me the briefest glance. "Definitely that one."

"You didn't even see the others," I say.

"Don't need to. You look too daring in that to even try the others on. Besides, I think you'd look good with a little punky pink eye shadow." The grin she gives me is kind of frightening. "Oh yes, I'm going to have a lot of fun painting your face."

"You scare me sometimes," I respond, giving myself another once-over in the mirror. I hate to admit it, but she has a point. I do look pretty daring in this. Seeing as this is my last night, I want to make an impression.

I work on my hair while she dries off and gets into her own outfit—it's a long black skirt with red carnation trim, along with a white blouse and red ringmaster coat that matches my own.

"Twinsies!" she shouts when she puts it on. We stand in the mirror together and admire ourselves. Our bright red and pink and purple clash like none other, but we do sort of match, and it looks pretty darn good. I'd never really wondered what a circus-themed dance would be like, but we definitely look the part.

She quickly throws some product in her hair and poufs it out into jaunty spikes, then expertly applies her own eyeliner and red and black eye shadow. When she's done, she looks like a punked-out pinup model, complete with bright strawberry lips and fake eyelashes. I didn't even try to do my own makeup while she got herself ready. I just watched her work and tried to remember what she did, in case I ever got the desire to try it myself.

"Okay," she says after twenty minutes of primping. "Your turn."

She brandishes her eyeliner brush like a weapon and gives me a devious grin. "Don't worry, this won't hurt a bit."

She kneels in front of me and brings the brush an inch from my eyelid. "Wait," she muses, "I thought that sounded wrong. This won't hurt *me* a bit. Yeah, that's right."

Then, with a giggle, she sets to work.

Chapter ☙ Twenty-Five

I thought that I knew what "nervous" meant. After a week of training and perform-ing in front of my peers, I thought I had a grasp of what going onstage entailed. But nothing was as bad as waiting for seven o'clock to roll around. Waiting for the dance was like waiting for a different sort of debut.

After all, it would be my first real dance with a real date. And if Luke decided to kiss me? My chest fluttered with the thought. Sure, maybe he wasn't Branden, but he was a pretty good guy. There were definitely worst first kisses out there.

"When does your boyfriend get here?" I ask Riley. She's doing what she always does when she has time to kill: She juggles.

"Sandy?" she asks.

"Yeah. Do you have more than one?"

She shakes her head. "One boyfriend is more than enough for me, thanks. He said he'd be here at seven, on the dot. So I guess I meet him down on the dance floor. I can't wait to get my boogie on."

"I don't think people actually say that anymore," I say. I examine my makeup for the millionth time. My eyes look *huge* with all this eye shadow. In a good way. Riley even pinned strands of my hair up.

"Well, *I* say it, and that's good enough for me." She chuckles. "You know, if you keep staring at your face like that, your makeup might just melt off."

I scowl at her.

"Nervous?" she asks.

"Obviously."

"Don't be. I have no doubt Luke is an excellent dancer. And after all the moving you've been doing this week, you will be too. As hard as it is to believe, you might actually, you know, *enjoy* this."

"That's just ridiculous," I say with a laugh. "You haven't rubbed off on me that much."

"Don't worry, there's still time." She pauses juggling and checks her checkerboard watch. "Speaking of, looks like we're on."

I look to my alarm clock. My stomach knots with fear. 6:59.

"Okay," I say. I take a deep breath and stand. "Let's do this."

Once more, the gym is completely transformed. Everything is cast in purple light and disco ball stars. Streamers hang from the rafters, balloons float in bunches along the wall. There are a dozen tables draped in white cloths and covered in candles on the edge of the dance floor. But no one's sitting at them, not like all the school dances I've attended. Everyone's already on the dance floor. My gut drops another level. Looks like there's no sitting this one out, even if I wanted to.

We stand in the doorway for a second, taking it all in. Then Riley gives a squeal and darts off toward the dance floor. She makes a wild leap and lands in the arms of a boy I immediately recognize as Sandy. Just like in the pictures Riley showed me, he's got mousy brown hair and a plethora of freckles. Only now he's wearing a suit that looks like it's a size too big. It makes his gangly frame appear even skinnier.

I glance away while they kiss. When I look back, she takes him by the hand and half drags him over to me.

"Sandy," she says, putting his hand in mine, "meet Jenn. She's my newest protégée. And also my best friend."

"Nice to meet you," he says. His handshake is surprisingly strong. I have a funny feeling he's one of those lithe guys, the ones who can secretly outlift most guys at the gym. "Riley's been telling me all about you."

I actually blush. "Really?"

She just shrugs. Then she grins, looking at something past my shoulder.

"Anyway," she says, bringing her attention back to me. "I believe you have someone waiting for you. Sandy, shall we dance?"

"But of course, my lady," he says. He bows to me, then guides Riley back to the dance floor.

I look to where Riley was gazing. Luke walks toward me, now only a few feet away.

"You look stunning," he says when he gets near. He's not in a suit like Sandy, but he's in smart black jeans and a lavender button-down shirt. His hair is slicked back, a few strands dangling at the side of his face.

"We match," I say, because being smooth around guys has never been my forte, and talking with Luke will probably never be seamless.

"I'm just going to pretend I planned it that way." He holds out his hand. "Care to dance?"

I take his hand and hope my palm isn't clammy from nerves. He grins at me and guides me to the dance floor.

The first few song are upbeat pop songs, and I do my best to move like I'm not an awkward girl who's only danced in public half a dozen times. For his part, Luke bobs along with me, barely taking his eyes off me. I can't help but blush every time I meet his gaze, so I try to focus on the people around me. Riley and Sandy are doing some silly dance moves to my left—pretty certain the one they're on now is called "the sprinkler"—and I spot Megan and Branden dancing together farther on. As usual, she's dancing way too close to him for my comfort, so I keep my eyes moving. Tyler and Kevin are dancing on my other side. They're both grinning and wearing button-down shirts and dark jeans. Kevin's in gray, Tyler's in blue. Luke follows my gaze.

"It's cool," he says over the music.

"What?" I ask. I look back to him.

"Them," he says, nodding to Tyler and Kevin. "You don't normally see that around here. It's nice that there's a place where they can be themselves."

I smile at him. He suddenly just won himself a dozen cool points in my book. "Agreed."

We dance for a few more songs, until I'm practically out of breath from all the bouncing. Riley comes over just then and takes my arm. "Mind if I steal her?" she asks Luke. "I need to go . . . what do they call it? Powder my nose."

Luke laughs. "Sure thing. Want something to drink?"

We both nod. "Yes, please."

Then Riley pulls me away, toward the bathroom, while Luke goes to the punch bowl.

"Okay," she says. "Damage report."

We're standing in front of the mirrors in the girls' bathroom, making sure no makeup has run since we started moving around.

"Damage report?"

"Yeah. Are you into him? Is he a crappy dancer? Do you need me to run interference?"

"Whoa, calm down," I say. "He's . . . actually pretty okay."

"So . . ."

"So," I say, shrugging, "we'll just see where the night goes."

"What about Branden?"

"What about him?"

"I saw you looking at him."

"I was trying not to."

She pats me on the shoulder. "Ignore him," she says. "Just enjoy your time with Luke. It's your last night."

My last night. The words are bittersweet. After tonight, there's no more practice, no more stress. No more Megan.

But also no more Riley or Tyler or Kevin.

"Promise we'll stay in touch?" I ask, because suddenly, keeping her as a friend seems much more important than Luke. She holds out her pinkie.

"Promise."

As we're heading back toward the gym, I run into the one person I really don't want to run into. Literally. Megan steps in front of me as I walk past, shoulder-checking me. I stop and spin around to face her. She doesn't look at me with any venom, though. In fact, the smile she gives is sickeningly sweet. She looks like a Parisian model, her hair pinned up and her bright-silver dress barely halfway down her thigh. I hate her for many reasons, not the least of which is the fact that she manages to pull that skimpy outfit off.

"Enjoying the dance?" she asks. There's so much sugar in her voice I could become diabetic.

Riley grabs my arm and tries to force me to move, but I don't. I'm going to fight fire with fire.

"Very much so. Luke is a perfect gentleman."

If anything, that just makes her smile grow.

"You're welcome," she says. Then she turns and walks away.

Riley's attempts at dragging me toward the gym succeed, and it's not until we're just outside the door that I let myself speak.

"What did she mean by that?"

"By what?" Riley asks.

"'You're welcome.'"

Riley shrugs. "She's just trying to get under your skin. Come on."

She pulls me the last few feet toward the door, but her words are far from comforting. As we head toward the table where Luke and Sandy are chatting, I have a sinking feeling that my suspicions about Luke were right.

Chapter ✺ Twenty-Six

I can't get rid of the little voice in the back of my head for the rest of the dance. It whispers at me through the pop songs that Luke is just using me. And when the music changes to a slow dance, the voice just gets louder. Luke steps up close to me and wraps his arms behind my waist, pulling me toward him. I have no choice but to place my arms around his neck. But I don't lean in, don't put my head on his chest like I've seen all those girls do in sappy romance movies. I keep a few inches of open air between us.

"You really are beautiful," he says.

"Thanks," I reply. I don't compliment him in return. The voice in my head becomes Megan's taunting drawl, and I can't shake the uncertainty that comes with it.

Sadly, he seems to mistake my silence and distant expression as something else. He leans in then, pulling me a little closer. His eyes flutter shut.

Alarm bells ring.

"Why did you ask me out?" I blurt.

His eyes snap open. "What?"

"Why did you ask me out?" I repeat.

"I don't understand—"

"You didn't start talking to me until right after the talent show. You could have any girl at camp, so why did you pick me?"

"Jenn, I—"

"Did Megan put you up to it?"

That makes him stutter. "Wh-What?"

I don't repeat myself. I just stare at him with what I hope is a no-nonsense look and wait for him to answer.

"Jenn, that's just ridiculous."

"You're not answering the question."

He shakes his head. "I shouldn't have to answer. You're being crazy."

"Then say she didn't put you up to it."

He opens his mouth. Nothing comes out. But there's a flicker in his features, the slightest tilt that tells me I've hit the nail on the head.

"Did she pay you?" I whisper. Even saying the words makes me feel sick.

Again, he says nothing.

"How much?" I push. We've both stopped dancing now. We

stand in the middle of the gym while everyone moves around us, and no one is aware of this minor breakdown. No one knows that inside, it feels like getting stood up all over again. But much, much worse.

Because I fell for it. Again.

"A hundred," he finally says.

I gasp. Take a step back.

"But I wasn't going to take it," he says. He tries to reach out for me, but I move out of the way. "I promise, Jenn. I was going to give it back."

"Which is it? You weren't going to accept it or you were going to return it? I'm not a trial date, Luke. I'm not a piece of clothing you can return."

He's gaping like a fish. The anger in me grows. I can't tell if it's rage at him or Megan or myself.

"You're disgusting," I finally say. Then I turn and run from the gym. The only consolation I have is that I don't start crying until I reach the dorms.

"Jennifer, wait!"

Riley's voice calls me to a stop. I'm halfway down the hall, heading toward our dorm room, where I'd planned on locking myself in the shower for the rest of the night. But hearing her voice makes me realize that I don't actually want to be alone. Not now. Not when it hurts this much.

"What happened?" she asks. She jogs up beside me and puts

her hands on my shoulders, examining me like she's expecting bruises. "What did he do?"

I wipe the tears from my eyes and try to choke down a sob.

"She paid him. She paid him to ask me."

"What? Who paid who?"

"Megan. She paid Luke to ask me to the dance. A hundred dollars."

Riley curses under her breath, calling Megan even worse things than before.

"I'm not going to let her get away with this," she whispers, almost to herself. Her cheeks aren't red, not yet, but they're slowly burning their way there. But the fight in me is gone. I feel broken and battered. I've given up.

"Riley, don't." I reach out and take her arm. She shrugs it off.

"No. No one treats my friends like this. She's going to pay."

Before I can beg her not to go, she stomps off down the hall. I consider going to our room for the briefest second, but the idea of letting Riley fight my battle is disgusting. I don't want this to end in violence. I just want this to end.

For the first time since that fateful audition on the flying trapeze, I want the camp to be over with.

I force down my tears and run to catch up to Riley just as she enters the gym.

But there's already a fight raging inside the gym. And it's immediately clear that this one has nothing to do with me.

The music screeches to a halt the moment we step into the

gym. The dance floor is a sea of yelling people crowding together. Riley gives me a questioning look, her features instantly dropping the anger from before.

Then we hear Tyler yelling above all the rest, and my anger switches to concern.

We run toward the huddle of people, pushing our way past everyone until we're in the center. Tyler and Kevin are locked in a fight with two guys I've never seen before. One swings at Kevin's face; Kevin dodges just in time and manages to shove the guy to the ground. Tyler is in a headlock. Only then do I register that Branden is there, trying to pull the guy's arms off Tyler's neck. It's immediately clear what it's about: the names the strangers are calling Tyler and Kevin make me sick.

I've heard people throw around the word "gay" in a derogatory way, but I've never heard it used like this.

"Stop it!" I scream, and I launch myself into the fray. Riley's right there beside me, but before either of us can get a swing in, the coaches bust through the crowd and grapple with the intruders. They pry the brown-haired boy off Tyler and yank the blond from the ground. Tyler and Kevin step back, chests heaving as the coaches detain the intruders. The unknown boys don't stop hurling insults, the least of which is that Tyler and Kevin are disgusting for dancing together.

"Get them out of here," Olga says. She pushes her way up behind me. "I don't care who they are, we will not tolerate this sort of behavior. The police are on their way."

The coaches detaining the strangers nod, then begin dragging the still-yelling boys toward the exit. The crowd parts away from them as they go.

"And you," Olga says, turning to us. I've always been a little intimidated by her, but she's never been this imposing. "What happened here?"

"They started it," Tyler pants. His arm is over Kevin's shoulders—I can't tell who is holding up who.

Kevin continues. "Just came up behind us and started punching."

"Are you hurt?" Olga asks.

Both boys shake their heads. Tyler manages a weak smile. "Should have known better than to mess with us. We'd have had them if they hadn't caught us by surprise."

"We don't condone violence here," Olga says. Then her voice softens. "But I'm glad you're okay. Leena? Take them to the nurse's station. Make sure they're fit to perform tomorrow. The rest of you, back to the dance."

Leena strides up and puts a comforting hand on each boy's shoulder. "Come on," she whispers, and begins to guide them away. Riley and I follow, Sandy at our heels.

As we pass through the crowd, I catch sight of Branden. His chest is heaving, and there's a bruise just beginning to form over his right eye. The look he gives me is filled with a thousand different emotions I can't begin to decipher. His lips mouth something.

It almost looks like *I'm sorry*.

Chapter ☻ Twenty-Seven

We spend the rest of the night with Tyler and Kevin in the nurse's station. Once Leena makes sure there's nothing wrong with the boys—like Tyler repeatedly says, the other guys didn't stand a chance—she leaves and brings us back a few tubs of ice cream.

"They were supposed to be for the dance," she says. "But I think you guys more than deserve it." Then she says she has to keep chaperoning, and that we can stay here until sign-in.

"Are you guys okay?" I ask the moment Leena's gone.

Tyler shrugs. "They didn't get a punch in."

"That's not what I mean."

Kevin sighs and leans in to Tyler. They're both sitting on the bed, sharing a pint of ice cream between them. "Nothing I haven't heard before," he says. "Sometimes that's the price of being yourself."

"I hate it," Riley mutters.

"Me too," Tyler says. "But the only way to change it is to challenge it."

And that's when I realize: They go through this every day. If they want to be themselves, they have to put up with bullying and abuse, both verbal and physical. The idea of it makes my blood boil and heart sink. Suddenly my problems seem insignificant.

"You're incredibly brave," I say. I don't mean to speak, but the words come out anyway.

"Thanks, love," Tyler says. He smiles, and when he speaks his tone is lighter. "You were pretty brave yourself, jumping in there like some warrior woman."

Kevin smiles as well. "Right? It's lucky the coaches jumped in when they did. You might have killed those guys."

"Given the chance," Riley mutters from the bench. Sandy pats her head.

"Calm down, warrior pixie," he says. "Violence is never the answer. Ice cream, on the other hand, is always the answer."

"Are you patronizing me?" she asks. There's no real anger in her voice.

"Um, no? Ice cream is the great equalizer. Unless you're lactose intolerant."

Riley just giggles and snuggles into him.

Even though I'm the fifth wheel, I don't feel awkward sitting on the chair alone. Being in this room with these people feels like being with family. All of us united because we're different, because at any moment life can throw a curveball.

Tears form in my eyes.

"What's wrong?" Kevin asks. "You're not lactose intolerant, are you?"

I sniff and smile. "No. It's just . . . you guys are probably the best friends I've ever had."

The words aren't enough to express the weight of it, the knowledge that if I ever needed something, they'd be there, and vice versa. Olga had said we'd grow to trust one another over the course of the camp, but I didn't know the full extent of it. I'd trust these guys with my life. And in many ways, being in a show with them, I already do. It's the most humbling and heartening thing I've ever felt.

"You're not so bad yourself," Riley says. "Now, less weepy, more ice creamy. You're smudging my masterpiece."

Leena comes back an hour or so later, right before sign-in. We spent the rest of our time in the office telling stories and figuring out our next big reunion. Which, if things go as hoped, will be in a few weeks.

"Who were they?" asks Tyler when Leena steps in.

"Just some guys from town," she says. "Thought they'd crash the party. Probably didn't think they'd be taken home in cop cars."

"Serves them right," Riley says. Sandy nudges her.

"I hope you don't mind," Leena says, looking at Tyler and

Kevin, "but we called your parents to let them know what happened. Well, we just told them that some guys came in and started a fight with you. We didn't give the specifics, just in case . . ."

"They know," Tyler says.

"Mine too," Kevin adds.

"Okay, well, we wanted to be on the safe side." She looks around the room. "Anyway, it's bedtime. Big day tomorrow."

And just like that, the final night at camp comes to a close. We head out of the room in silence, toward the dorms, following Leena. Tyler and Kevin are holding hands in some quiet show of resilience. Sandy has his arm looped around Riley's shoulder, and her hand is in mine. She squeezes my fingers like she, too, knows the emotional weight of this. When Leena tells Sandy he needs to head home, he kisses Riley on the top of the head and leaves, promising he'll be there front and center for the show tomorrow. For some reason, this just makes my heart drop a little more; Mom and Dad will be there for the show, sure. But I don't have anyone special coming to see me—no friends or boyfriend. Even as the four of us walk down the hall together, I can't shake the feeling of being alone.

The boys give us hugs good night, and then Riley and I head up to our room. No one else is mingling in the halls. I've no clue if the dance is still going on or if we're just getting back late. Something tells me it's the latter. We don't speak as we scrub off our makeup and change into pajamas. My brain is racing the entire time; I'm more nervous about going to sleep and saying good-bye to this than I was coming here. And that's saying something.

It's not until we're both in bed and the lights are off that Riley speaks.

"Well," she says, almost to herself. "That was an eventful night."

I don't respond; I keep my eyes closed as I relive the night. I hear her turn over in bed.

"You okay?" she asks.

Again, I don't respond.

"Is this about Luke?" she asks. Her voice goes softer; she knows this isn't a subject I want to discuss.

"Yes and no," I say. "I just . . . I feel so stupid. I can't believe I fell for it again. But it's not a big deal, not compared to what Tyler and Kevin went through. So that just makes me feel even worse."

"You can't do that to yourself. You're allowed to feel hurt at what Luke did to you, no matter what's going on in anyone else's life."

I shrug.

"It doesn't matter," I say. "After tomorrow I won't see Luke ever again."

Riley goes silent for a moment.

"You know, he was asking about you. Branden."

"What? When?"

"Sandy told me. Branden came up to him when he saw you run out. He wanted to make sure you were okay."

I'd been doing my best to force the image of Branden out of

my mind. Her words just bring it all back. *Why* am I still attracted to him? *Why* do I still care? Still, knowing he was thinking of me makes me feel a little warmer.

"Then why didn't he ask me himself?" I mutter.

"I don't know. Maybe he was worried it would upset you more?" She sighs. "I still don't think Branden's a bad guy. I mean, I was watching him dance with Megan. He did *not* seem into it at all. In fact, he looked like he wanted out. And I definitely caught him staring at you. A lot."

"It doesn't matter."

"I'm just saying," she continues, "Megan paid Luke to ask you out. If she's willing to stoop that low, who knows what she did or said to Branden to make him go for her."

I hadn't thought of it like that. *Had* Megan manipulated Branden somehow? Was she the real bad guy in all of this?

"We'll probably never know," I say after a while. "Anyway, I'm tired. I'll see you in the morning."

She whispers a good night. I can tell she wants to press the subject, but she doesn't. For that, I'm grateful.

I pull the covers tight around me and curl up. I know I should be thinking of Tyler and Kevin and their struggles. I know I should give up on the whole dating thing. But as I lie there, all I can think of is the look Branden gave me when Leena took us away. He said he was sorry. For what?

I don't have any answers, and as sleep folds in, I'm pretty certain my dreams won't either.

Chapter ✎ Twenty-Eight

The next morning is a rush of nerves and excitement. Despite the crazy of the dance last night, all Tyler and Kevin talk about over breakfast is their act and how they can fine-tune the moves. Neither Riley nor I mention anything about the fight. If the boys are over it, we will be as well. So she and I talk about our own routine and the show in general and occasionally mention the next time we're going to meet up. Having her as a friend just furthers my desire to get a driver's license and car.

After breakfast is another run-through of the show, this one in full dress. Riley and I get into our costumes—a mismatch of tie-dye and neon colors, just like the rest of the jugglers, and head to the backstage area behind the tent. Yesterday was our one chance of seeing the show; today we rehearse like there's actually an audience.

Because in a few hours, the bleachers are going to be packed.

Once we're all assembled in the grass behind the tent, Olga comes out and makes a few announcements about show order and music cues. Someone nudges into me while she's talking. I glance over, expecting it to be Riley returning from a prop-gathering mission, and see Branden.

For a moment he just stands there, silent, looking at me with an expression I can't quite place.

"Hey," he finally whispers.

"Hi," I whisper back.

"I need to talk to you."

I glance over to Olga, who's finishing up her notes. He takes my cue.

"After?" he asks.

I shrug. I don't know what he wants to talk about, but I can't forget Riley's words last night. I also can't ignore the little bubble of hope inside of me when he's near.

"Okay," he says. "Well, break a leg."

He seems torn up when he says it, but before I can say anything, he vanishes back into the crowd. Olga's done with her notes. Showtime.

The show is a blur. Riley appears beside me just in time to dash out onstage for the *charivari*. We do our routine, and after what feels like no time at all, we dash back behind the scenes and out into the grass. I half expect Branden to show up and try to chat with me, but he doesn't. He stays over beside his acro group. I catch Luke's eye and glare. He blushes and looks away.

Riley and I practice our act over and over backstage. There's nothing else to do, really, and warming up like this keeps my mind off other things. Like Megan, stretching beside the tent with her sisters. If I think about her too much, I may just "accidentally" chuck a juggling club at her head.

Surprisingly, I'm not nearly as nervous as I thought I'd be this time around. Maybe it's because the practice keeps my brain engaged on not losing an eye. Maybe it's because I'm actually starting to get used to this performing thing. Whatever the reason, I barely notice the time fly by. Then, out of nowhere, Olga comes back and says that we're skipping intermission for this run-through. Riley and I take our places. Then, with the blare of music, we run onstage.

Our act goes off without a hitch. The lights blind me with brilliance, and music pulses in my veins. We make every pass, hit every cue. When we finally run offstage, I feel like a rock star. The sensation lasts for the next few acts, while Riley and I sit out back and chat with Tyler and Kevin. I could really get used to this show-business thing and can only imagine it will be a hundred times better with real, live applause.

After what seems like no time at all, we head back onstage for the finale. Everything is perfect. By the time we take our bows, I'm covered in a light sheen of sweat and can practically feel myself glowing with happiness. I take Riley's hand for the bow. *This* is where I'm meant to be. Under the spotlights, surrounded by friends. This is what performing is all about.

As we head offstage, I realize that that was our last time to practice. The next time I set foot in the ring, I'll be surrounded by an audience.

A few days ago, that thought would have terrified me. Today it just makes me excited.

We change out of our costumes and grab a quick lunch before families start to arrive. Our conversations are light, completely glossing over the fact that in a few hours, we're going to be heading our separate ways. For now, there's still a show to run. There's still some time in the spotlight.

A part of me expects Branden to approach during lunch, but he doesn't come near. The only consolation is that Megan isn't with him. She stays at a table with her sisters. I feel a little vindicated in that, but also a little bad: Being mean to people has never been my strength, and seeing her so outside the troupe almost makes me want to go up and chat with her. All her manipulating and meanness have set her apart from the company. I glance around at my table, at Riley, who grins and chucks celery stalks at Tyler and Kevin, neither of whom are very good at catching the flying food in their mouths. Probably because they can't stop laughing.

I smile. In that moment, I know I got out of this camp precisely what I wanted: I found a family of friends. I'm getting my time in the spotlight. Sure, not the way I thought, but it's still fantastic.

Now, if only Branden had asked me out in the first place . . .

After lunch we head back to our rooms to pack. I've never liked packing, even for vacation—it always feels like saying good-bye. Thankfully, Riley blares some cheesy pop music while we pack, so the experience isn't so bad. We dance around and sing at the top of our lungs and throw our unfolded clothes in our bags. Leena comes in at one point; I expect her to tell us to turn the music down. Instead she sings along to the chorus, with my hairbrush as a microphone. Then she bows, tells us we need to be backstage in twenty minutes, and leaves.

Riley and I exchange a glance.

"Time for one more song?" she asks.

"Always," I say.

And she plays the song we did for the talent show. I've never sung so loud in my life.

We're backstage. I haven't been out to see if my parents are there in the audience; I kind of don't want to know. But I've been back here for the last ten minutes, watching people filter into the tent from the corner of my eye. Riley's kept us practicing the entire time. Like everyone else, we're in full costume and makeup. And like everyone else, we have nothing to do now except run our routine over and over and pump ourselves up for our first, last, and only show.

Finally, once everyone's in the tent, Olga comes out back and has us assemble.

"All right, campers," she says. She's dressed in full ringmaster regalia, including a red coat and a black top hat. "I don't have much to say—it's already been said. You've put in so much heart and hard work over the last few days; no matter how today's show goes, you should all be very proud of yourselves for what you've accomplished. Six days ago you didn't even know one another. Today you have created a show as a team. You're a family now, and if there's one thing I've learned in this industry, it's that a circus family stays with you for life.

"So let's go out there and show everyone what you've accomplished. Let's give them a show they'll remember forever!"

She cheers, and we all join in. My nerves are dancing and my heart pounds, but it's with excitement and adrenaline. It's showtime. I glance at Riley, who gives me a huge smile. I look to Tyler and Kevin, who are hugging each other.

Time to show my family the new family I've just made.

There's no way to describe how it feels to run onstage with a full audience cheering you on. I've never felt so exhilarated, so alive. When we bow after our final pose of the *charivari* and the crowd explodes into applause, I almost cry with happiness. At that moment, I know this is what I was made for. No matter what, I'm coming back next year. Better than ever. I won't let this be my last time onstage.

The music and applause is a constant through the rest of the first act. Riley and I practice our routine and don't drop a single pass. Then, just like during the rehearsal that morning, the first act ends almost as quickly as it started. My heart beats faster—our act is up after intermission.

Although Olga said we're allowed to mingle with our parents, I stay backstage. For some reason, it makes it feel like I'm keeping this dream alive. Once I talk to my mom and dad, I'm back to being normal old Jennifer. So long as I stay back here, I'm still the circus star. Riley leaves to go say hi to Sandy, so I stay in the back and practice my solo passes.

What I don't expect is for Megan to come up to me. She storms over in her silver leotard, and for a moment I think she's going to punch me. Her hands are clenched at her sides, and she's giving me a death glare. Her sisters are right behind her.

"I hope you're happy," Megan fumes.

"I don't know what you're talking about," I say.

"Leave off it, Megan," Sara says. "This isn't a game. You've already done enough."

"Yeah," says her other sister. Olivia, I think her name is. "It's the last day. Just leave her alone."

"No," Megan says. She shakes off her sisters and storms up to me. "He was supposed to choose *me*. Don't you see that? It was always supposed to be this way: He was supposed to see me again and remember he loved me." That's when I realize there are actually tears in her eyes.

"C'mon," Sara says. She reaches out again. "Just forget him, okay?"

"Yeah," Olivia agrees. She takes Megan's other arm.

"I hate you," Megan says. "You aren't *good enough.*"

But before I can get a question in, Olivia is guiding her distraught sister away. Sara lingers behind for a moment.

"Sorry about that," she says. "About everything. She and Branden dated at camp two years back. He broke up with her. She's been plotting this for a while—it's half the reason she dragged us to this camp in the first place."

"Oh," I say. "I'm . . . sorry."

She shrugs. "I've gotten used to it. Anyway, break a leg."

"Thanks," I say, and watch her follow her sisters to the front of the tent.

"Huh," I murmur to myself. That was definitely not what I expected. I actually feel a little sorry for Megan. Well, for her sisters, at least. I wonder if she's that demanding at home. *She made them go to camp so she could hook up with Branden?* No wonder she seemed so desperate.

I glance around, half expecting to see Branden come over and finally tell me whatever it was he wanted to say. But he's nowhere to be seen. Must be out front with his parents.

Riley comes back a little while later. Almost on cue, the music in the tent changes.

"Are you ready?" she asks.

I smile. "Born ready."

She gives me a quick hug. Then, when the cue hits, we run onstage.

Our act goes perfectly. When I'm in the spotlight, I'm no

longer Jennifer. I'm a star, an actor on a glorious stage. When we finish in what seems like only heartbeats later, I feel connected to this place in a way I could never imagine before. Applause fills me. I take Riley's hand and bow deeply, convinced I can hear my parents yelling high above the rest of the crowd. Then we run offstage.

The rest of the show is a blur.

In no time at all we're gathering for the finale, Riley's hand firmly in mine and a grin plastered on both our faces. We run out into the ring, and the troupe performs its final act. The crowd doesn't stop clapping, not for the entire routine. Not until Olga comes out and thanks the parents for letting us be part of such an amazing experience.

"Now," she says, "we'd like to extend the circus experience to you, the families who have supported us. For the next hour, our coaches will be on hand to teach you whatever skills you'd like to try out, from juggling to the flying trapeze rig out back." She looks behind her to us, and I swear her eyes catch on me. She grins. "This extends to our performers as well, just in case they wanted one last shot at a new skill."

My heart leaps. Riley's grip tightens on mine.

Olga's giving me a second chance.

I could try the flying trapeze again.

Before I can get lost in the thought, the troupe dashes offstage. Behind the tent, everyone is hugging and congratulating one another as parents and family members come back to offer their own praise. I spot my parents and run over to them, wrapping them both in a hug.

"You were amazing, Jennifer!" my dad says. My mom echoes this, squeezing me tight.

"Thanks, guys," I say. I look to the flying trapeze. "Before we go, there's something I've gotta do."

They don't ask what I mean, just give me another hug and let me run off. I head straight to the flying trapeze. Time to face my fears.

Chapter Twenty-Nine

All the coaches are already there, along with a handful of families. Only a few other kids from the camp are there, still in makeup and costume.

The moment I see the rig, my heart does a little somersault and the fear comes back. *You can't do that. You're too much of a coward. It's too high—you'll just panic again and make a fool of yourself in front of all these people.*

But that voice doesn't last very long. It can't, not under the pressure of the new strength I've found. I was just onstage performing in front of a live audience. My act went perfectly. And now, here I am, given a second chance just like Riley said. I'm not going to blow this. I'm going to prove to everyone, once and for all, that Jennifer Hayes is not a coward: I'm a circus star.

I step up to the front of the crowd—no one's forming a line—and offer to go first. Tanya looks at me with a small smile on her face. She remembers me trying the trapeze before, I know it. But rather than smiling like she's laughing inside, her grin is comforting. Proud, almost. She straps the safety belt around my waist.

"You know the drill," she says, putting a hand on my shoulder. She leans over. "You can do this," she whispers. Then she lets me go.

I stare up at the ladder, the height that has haunted me for the last week. It seems to represent everything I've been through, every time I've given up or failed. My hand shakes as I reach out and take hold of the first rung. The small voice inside of me is telling me to give up now, before I take that first step, before I find out just how much of a coward I really am.

I ignore the voice. I climb.

I don't look down as I climb up the shaky rope ladder. It sways slightly as my weight shifts, and a knot of vertigo lodges in my throat. But I don't stop, not even when I reach the point where I gave up last time. I don't look down or let that voice take hold until I reach the very top, where one of the coaches waits with a hand outstretched. When I'm on the tiny wooden platform that feels like it's a hundred feet above the ground, I look out to the tent and the crowd below me.

What a rush! Everything is spread out and tiny. I see my mom and dad down there, waving at me. Riley and Sandy, both of them jumping up and down with excitement. Tyler and Kevin, hand in hand, cheering. Leena's there beside them, calling out that I can do it. And I even see Branden, standing a little ways apart, looking up at me with an expression I can't quite see.

The coach snaps the safety lines to my belt and pulls the trapeze back for me.

"Just hold on and try to beat your body when she tells you to," he says. "And when she says let go, just let go. Keep your arms flat at your sides—don't try to land on hands and knees. Got it?"

I nod. I can't stop looking at the view. It's gorgeous up here. Even the air seems cleaner, clearer. Suddenly I can't understand why I was so scared before. Everything from up here seems so *perfect*.

"Okay," I say. I reach out and take the trapeze in both hands. The taped metal is cool. The coach holds on to the back of my belt as I lean out, staring across the rig and down at the ground that seems so far away. My heart hammers. My palms go cold. But I'm here. I'm here. And I'm not backing down now.

"Ready?" he asks.

I nod.

"On three. One. Two. Three!"

I leap out. The world soars.

An excited yell leaves my lips as I sway over the net, wind whipping in my face and the sun shining bright. I feel like a bird, like a superhero. I arc out and swing back, nearly reaching the platform I was just on. I can barely hear the coach calling out for me to beat over my laughter. When the swing finally slows to a near halt and she tells me to release, I'm giddy with adrenaline. I let go. The ground plummets toward me, the net catches me and bounces me up a few feet like a trampoline. For a few seconds I just lie there, bouncing up and down. Then I grab the edge of the net and roll down, my eyes squeezed shut. Someone helps me down. I expect it to be the coach.

It's Branden.

"You were . . . you were amazing." His words are breathy, filled with excitement. The coach comes over and helps me out of my safety belt, but I barely notice it. Branden doesn't move away, doesn't stop looking at me. I see Riley from the corner of my eye, but she gives me space. She also keeps my parents back.

"Jenn, I'm sorry," Branden continues. "About the dance, about everything. I never wanted to go with Megan, but she said you weren't interested in me and like Luke instead. She pretty much forced me to ask her."

My jaw drops.

"She told me you weren't interested in me," I say. "And her sister said you guys made out the night of the talent show."

He shakes his head. "I'd never do that. That was a lie. She and I were never a thing—I've been trying to convince her of that since camp two years ago. I like you, Jenn. I really, really like you. I've wanted it to be you all along."

My heart flutters with his words, but they're tinged with sadness.

"I wasted all camp trying to work up the nerve to ask you out," he continues. "I thought I was going to lose you when

220

Luke asked you to the dance. Then I heard what he and Megan did. . . . I can't believe it, Jenn. I'd never hurt you like that. Ever. And then, today, seeing you face your fears, and watching you defend your friends last night, well, you inspired me. I need to face my own fears."

He looks me deep in the eyes then. It feels like he's actually seeing me for who I am, and not just the girl I try to be.

"I know camp is over," he whispers, "but I'd really like a chance at this. We live pretty close to each other. I think it could work. Would you . . . would you like to try? Going out with me, I mean?"

I gasp.

I don't even think about my answer.

"Yes," I say. "Yes, I will."

He smiles, the warm sunlight playing off his lips. His arms wrap around my waist, pull me tight.

And when he leans in to kiss me, it feels like flying all over again.

My entire body ached as I stretched each limb and popped my back, trying to shake off the effects of the long, long trip. Cleveland to New York to London to here—I still couldn't believe we'd left home yesterday afternoon and had just arrived in Edinburgh's airport a couple of hours ago.

But as I stared out our hotel window overlooking Princes Street, with Scotland's rolling greens and ancient buildings staring back at me, the stiffness in my body faded away. I was really here. And it was breathtaking so far. I couldn't wait to see what other sights Scotland held.

There was a lovely park area in front of our hotel with rich green grasses and trees, and beyond the park there were rows of ancient-looking buildings lined along the street, pressed side by side with pubs, shops, and churches. This whole city was steeped in history. I was crazy excited to explore.

My mom stepped behind me and gave a soft sigh. "It's gorgeous, isn't it?"

I nodded my agreement. "Well worth being cramped in an airplane for this." I'd spent hours last week scouring online to find pictures, videos, anything to help get me ready for our two-week vacation to Scotland. But nothing could have prepared me for the image before me.

Downtown Edinburgh bustled with people below, and music and noise filtered up to us from the packed streets. I couldn't help but smile as I watched. Excitement swelled, and I was suddenly itching to get out there and walk. I wanted to touch the warm bricks with my fingers, smell the pub food and flowers, and hear the noises up close and personal.

"Ava," my dad said from behind me, "I printed you a copy of our itinerary. There's also a backup on your bedside table."

Mom chuckled, and we turned and faced my dad. He didn't show any signs of fatigue, since he'd slept like a log on our flight from New York to London last night. I, on the other hand, had gotten intermittent sleep, due to the snoring man on my right who apparently couldn't snooze unless his head was tilted my way.

Mom and I sat down on my bed, and we dutifully took our copies of the papers while Dad recited an overall rundown of how the trip would go. First we would spend a few days in Edinburgh and the surrounding cities, and Dad would spend some of that time doing research on our family heritage. Then we were taking a weeklong bus trip through Oban, Inverness, and St. Andrews so we could explore the Scottish Highlands.

The more he talked, the more excited he got, his eyes flashing bright.

"And if we stick to this schedule, we'll have plenty of time to fit in almost everything the experts agree we need to see," he concluded with a flourish. "We'll experience a good portion of what Scotland has to offer."

"This sounds like a pretty thorough sightseeing plan you've crafted. But do we get to sleep anytime in there?" Mom asked, her lips quirking with quiet amusement. "And maybe have a dinner or two as well?"

He rolled his eyes. "Don't be ridiculous. Of course we do. I scheduled an hour for each meal—it's listed clearly under each day."

An hour? Yeah, right. Mom was the slowest eater in the world. Apparently, he'd forgotten about this little fact. "Good luck policing Mom's eating speed," I told him with a hearty chuckle.

She shot me a mock glare, then grabbed her phone. Her fingers flew over the screen as she typed. "Laugh it up, smarty-pants. I just believe in savoring my meals. Anyway, I'm sending Mollie a text to let her know we've arrived. I'm so excited to see her. It's been far too many years since she and I have hung out."

During our travels here, Mom had given me some information about this family we were hanging out with in Scotland.

Apparently, Mom and Mollie had been best friends in high school. After they'd graduated and moved on to college, Mollie had spent a semester in Scotland her senior year. She'd fallen head over heels in love—both with the land and with a handsome guy she'd met on campus. The decision to stay here had been hard, but she hadn't looked back.

Mollie's family still lived in the Cleveland area, and Mom said she had coffee with her parents every once in a while. But Mollie herself hadn't been back to visit in years.

The way Mom talked about Mollie reminded me of my friendship with Corinne. Lasting and strong, no matter what happened in life. We'd known each other for years and had grown into best friends fast. Before I'd left for this vacation, she'd demanded I send her lots of pictures of my trip and keep her up to date on all the cute guys I saw. If only she could have come with me to experience Scotland too. She would love what I'd seen so far; the old buildings and rolling greens would appeal to her artistic nature. Talk about inspiration.

"So, Dad, where are you going to start your research?" I asked. He'd joined an ancestry website last year to begin building our family tree, and it was cool to see the old scanned birth certificates, pictures, and other artifacts regarding our ancestors.

"The National Archives of Scotland." He dug through his suitcase and produced a battered notebook. As he flipped through the pages, I saw his signature scrawl filling at least the first half of the notebook. Dad was nothing if not thorough and methodical.

"It'll get me a good start on which town we should narrow our focus down to. And someone online mentioned I can check out local churches as well, since they keep meticulous birth and death records."

After interviewing a number of family members and confirming the information online, Dad had traced our family line back to Scotland. When he'd casually brought up the idea of continuing his research in person, Mom and I had begged him for a family trip there until he'd caved. We'd all figuratively tightened our belts and cut back on spending to make sure we could afford it, with no complaints.

Yeah, I was willing to follow any goofy, overplanned agenda Dad set if it meant experiencing this. Even our hotel felt cool and different and older than anything I'd seen in America. This country breathed history, and I was full of anticipation to take pictures and draw it.

"Will we be able to find out our family tartan?" I asked him. It would be so cool to get a kilt made in it. Corinne would die of jealousy if I wore it to visit her—and probably tease me a little too.

He shrugged. "If we have one, I don't see why not. I don't think all Scottish families do, but maybe we'll be lucky."

My stomach growled, and I clapped my hands over it with a chagrined laugh. "Sorry."

Mom quirked her crooked smile and put her phone away. "Someone's hungry, it seems."

"Well, it has been a few hours since we ate lunch," I protested.

And even that had been a little lackluster—a plain sandwich and chips. I wanted a real dinner.

Dad scrunched up his mouth as he thought. "Well, we're not actually scheduled to start exploring Edinburgh until tomorrow, but I suppose we could get a taste of its foods right now and maybe do a little shopping—"

"Yes!" Mom and I said together, then laughed. We jumped off the bed and stood in front of Dad with pleading eyes.

He gave a heavy, resigned sigh. "Okay, fine. Put on your jackets, and let's go grab a meal. There's a place on High Street that was recommended by a number of people. We'll get some authentic Scottish cuisine there."

I slipped on my dark-blue fleece jacket and checked myself out in the mirror. My blond bob was a bit worse for wear but not horribly so, and a quick run-through of my brush smoothed the strays. I had on jeans and a T-shirt. Not my foxiest outfit ever, but it would do for now.

"You look lovely, Ava," Mom said as she walked by me, giving my upper arm a small squeeze.

We left the room and made our way down the hall, down the stairs, and into the large wood-trimmed lobby. A variety of people hustled and bustled around us, checking in as they dragged suitcases to the front desk, talking, laughing. Their energy was infectious, and I found my spirits lifted even higher.

Wow, I was in Scotland—I was really here! And this was going to be an awesome two weeks.

"Oh, just to remind you," Mom said to me when we stepped outside into the mild summer air. "Mollie and Steaphan have a son around your age. He'll be hanging out with us too. Graham," she added with a broad smile.

My good mood slipped a touch, and a hint of wariness filled me. Wonderful. Mom's attempts at vacation matchmaking weren't very subtle.

We crossed Princes Street and headed down the sidewalk toward High Street, weaving through the crowds of people. The air carried the rich scents of food and the sounds of drummers off in the distance. Sunlight peeked through intermittent clouds and warmed the air, which hovered around the midsixties. When we'd left Cleveland yesterday, it had been in the nineties and scorching hot for days. This was far, far more comfortable.

"I'm sure Graham is a nice guy," I finally said to Mom. My stomach growled again. I focused on my hunger in an attempt to change the subject. "So, I can't wait to try this restaurant. Do you think you'll try haggis while we're here? I don't know if I'm brave enough to eat it."

Mom ignored my food ramblings and continued, "You should give him a chance, Ava. I've seen Graham's pictures, and he's quite handsome. A clean-cut boy with a friendly smile."

"I'm sure he is." I knew the grin on my face was super fake, but I flashed it anyway. A mother's idea of handsome was quite different from a daughter's. Plus, I tended to like guys who were a little less prim and proper. David's short, scruffy black hair and dark-brown eyes came to mind, and I shoved the memory right back out again. At least that old sting in my heart didn't flare up at the thought of him, the way it had for so long after our breakup earlier this year.

Dad, who was already in tourist mode, had his camera at the ready and was busy snapping shots of the large brick and stone buildings lining the street. I took out my phone and snapped a few shots so I could send them to Corinne.

Mom nudged me with her shoulder and gave me a wistful smile. She was such a romantic. "I know what you're thinking, Ava, but who knows? Graham might turn out to be your Scottish vacation romance. After all, Mollie hadn't planned on falling in love, but here she is, almost twenty years later and still happy as a lark."

I gave her a casual shrug. Yeah, it would be awesome to find someone I liked that much, but I wouldn't hold my breath. I'd liked David too, a lot, and that had turned out terribly. No one else knew what had happened between us to make us break up, not even Corinne, and I wanted to keep it that way. The truth was far too mortifying. "We'll see," I replied with a broad smile. "I'm looking forward to meeting them all." That much was accurate, at least.

We turned the corner and headed down High Street. I couldn't stop staring, absorbing the sights of Old Town Edinburgh. The buildings were packed side by side with adorable storefronts in brilliant colors. Rich Scottish accents poured from young and old guys sitting at pub tables as they talked faster than I could understand, pints in hand. Everywhere I looked I saw tartan patterns on clothing and even a few men in kilts. Their bare calves were strong and sturdy, covered with hair.

A couple of blocks down, Dad led us into a small restaurant with huge glass windows. A waitress with wildly curly gray hair and a warm face seated us and gave us menus. I scoured mine a little hesitantly at first but realized I recognized a lot of the food available and felt a strong sense of relief. An embarrassed flush crept up my cheeks. If my mom could read my thoughts right now, she'd make a pointed comment about me always making assumptions.

Mom and Dad ordered, and I got the sausage-and-mash bake—couldn't go wrong with potatoes and sausage. My parents talked about tomorrow's plans with Mollie and Steaphan, and I let my gaze wander around the room. The top half was blue wallpaper, while the bottom was wood-trimmed with neat tables lined up along the walls. It was cozy and lovely.

And the air smelled heavenly. I couldn't wait to eat.

"—excited to find out where we're really from," Dad was saying. "I should be able to search all the way back to our home village, even." He suspected our heritage could be traced way back to the Middle Ages, based on something he'd found online, and was hoping to confirm it with in-person research.

Our meals were delivered fast, and the food was every bit as good as I'd hoped it would be. I polished off my whole plate in record time. My parents got fish and fries—uh, chips, as our waitress called them.

We paid our bill and left the restaurant, then spent a couple of hours strolling along High Street to window-shop a bit. I was tempted to buy a bunch of stuff, but I didn't want to spend all my money on the first day.

The temperature had dropped a few degrees, and I zipped my fleece up a touch. Crazy how much hotter Ohio was than Scotland. Good thing Mom and I had done our research beforehand and had packed appropriate clothing.

As the sun began to sink into the horizon, we made our way back to our hotel. My eyes were gritty and I was a bit sluggish. Mom was walking slower too, and even Dad's enthusiasm was starting to fade. Fatigue definitely hit us hard after that big meal.

Still, I wasn't quite ready to go to sleep yet. When we got inside, I begged to explore the hotel a bit. Mom and Dad reluctantly agreed. I grabbed a room key and took off before they could change their mind.

The building was old, and all its little details mesmerized me as I walked up and down the halls, trailing my fingers along the walls. Spindly metal wall sconces glowed with golden lamplight. Ornate wallpaper covered the halls in subtle patterns I could feel under my fingertips, and the carpeted halls were worn but soft. I was tempted to kick off my shoes and dig my toes in the plush brown nap.

There were a few modern, updated rooms in the hotel's first floor as well, for business conferences, I assumed, bearing massive slabs of tables and sleek chairs. The dining hall was a large, blue-carpeted room with dark wooden tables in intimate clusters and small candles in the center of each smooth surface. The space invited people to come in and linger for a while. I needed to ask Mom and Dad if we could eat there tomorrow. Even though I was full, the rich scents of cooking food from the nearby kitchen tempted me to eat more.

When I got back to the lobby, I noticed a group of guys standing together. There was a mix of accents tangling—Irish, English, even German. One English guy had a shock of blond hair and stood a good foot taller than the rest. Super handsome. It was so tempting to take a quick picture to send to Corinne, but I didn't want to look too obvious. But I made a mental note to tell her about it.

I headed upstairs, tiptoed into the room—my folks were already asleep—got ready for bed, then conked out almost before my head hit the pillow.

A. DESTINY is the coauthor of the Flirt series. She spends her time reading, writing, and watching sweet romance movies. She will always remember her first kiss.

ALEX R. KAHLER is one of those individuals who can't sit still for very long, unless, of course, he's writing. In the past few years he's traveled from Seattle to Scandinavia for school and circus training. Because yes, when he isn't writing or on the road, he works in the circus arts as an aerialist and assistant. He's a big believer that if you want to do something, the only person stopping you is yourself. He is also an author for teens and adults, writing under the name A. R. Kahler. You can learn more about him and his travels at ARKahler.com.